ALL OUR BRAVE, EARTHLY SCARS

Danielle Lim is an award-winning author of three books.

Her short story collection, *And Softly Go the Crossings*, won the Book of the Year as well as Best Literary Work in the Singapore Book Awards 2021. Her novel, *Trafalgar Sunrise*, was shortlisted for Best Literary Work in the Singapore Book Awards 2019. Her memoir, *The Sound of SCH: A Mental Breakdown, a Life Journey*, won the Singapore Literature Prize 2016 (non-fiction), and has been translated to Chinese and Tamil, published in Taiwan and India.

The Publishers Weekly (US) listed Danielle as one of Singapore's top writers in 2016. Her works have been featured in *The Straits Times, BiblioAsia*, CNA938 and ABC Radio Australia, in *The West Australian* and other publications. She has been invited to speak at various local and international events, including the Singapore Writers Festival, the Kimberley Writers Festival, and the George Town Literary Festival.

Danielle is an alumna of the University of Oxford and resides in Singapore, where she is a lecturer.

Also by Danielle Lim
And Softly Go the Crossings, 2020

Advance Praise for *All Our Brave, Earthly Scars*

'Against a backdrop of loss and the violence of repeated fiery destruction, this sensitive and moving novel explores how life scars and reforms us in the deepest ways. Through the cycle of annihilation and regeneration in both the personal lives of her characters and in the larger social context, Danielle Lim perceptively explores the inner dynamics of relationships, and lays bare the pains and the courage demanded of us all on life's uncertain journey.'

—Meira Chand, author of *Sacred Waters*

'Danielle Lim shows her mastery of craft in her second novel: Layered storytelling spanning decades, and prose that cuts the air with its sheer poetry. Magnificent and worth re-reading!'

—Felix Cheong, author of *Sprawl: A Graphic Novel*

'With writing that is breathtakingly moving, Danielle Lim weaves a gut-wrenching story of characters drawn to each other by fierce loves but pulled apart by walls created by their parents' generation. Against a backdrop of real historical events like the Bukit Ho Swee fire that swept through Singapore and the 2002 Bali bombing, it is a drama of intense emotions that left me reeling at times. Yet by the end, the spirit triumphs, and there is hope for the future, even if it is tinged by past sorrows and upheavals.'

—Tara Dhar Hasnain, literary editor and lecturer

'A touching and riveting story. Danielle Lim weaves in the little-known fact of how burn injuries can have a life-changing impact on burn victims and their families, and how scars can remain even years later.'

—Dr Chong Si Jack, President, Association for Burn Injuries Singapore

All Our Brave, Earthly Scars

Danielle Lim

PENGUIN BOOKS
An imprint of Penguin Random House

PENGUIN BOOKS

USA | Canada | UK | Ireland | Australia
New Zealand | India | South Africa | China | Southeast Asia

Penguin Books is part of the Penguin Random House group of companies
whose addresses can be found at global.penguinrandomhouse.com

Published by Penguin Random House SEA Pte Ltd
9, Changi South Street 3, Level 08-01,
Singapore 486361

First published in Penguin Books by Penguin Random House SEA 2022
Copyright © Danielle Lim 2022

ISBN 9789815017106

Typeset in Garamond by MAP Systems, Bangalore, India

www.penguin.sg

For my husband and children

We are each of us angels with only one wing,
And we can only fly by embracing one another.
—Luciano De Crescenzo

Zero

***

2002

Bali, Indonesia

Chapter 1

Darkness has slumped over the town of Kuta.

Black feathers of smoke rise on outstretched wings, carrying with them silent, hollowed out prayers towards the darkened heavens above. A burnt white dove hovering in the air.

The streetlamps shed their tears of light amid sheaths of burning heat so intense it is as if for a moment, there is only a vacuum of impassioned anger.

A two-legged armchair has sunk to its knees, its smooth wood now charred, its arms offering memories of bygone greetings and chatter. The open arms can now only show forth an avalanche of twisted metal, shattered glass, blown out dreams, and bleeding lives.

Two firefighters shout to their comrades as they carry a blackened body out of the blaze. Blood is splattered on the ground, on the debris, on ripped cars. Dead bodies lie everywhere.

The sound of spraying water offered by the arms of the firefighters brings a cool, misty balm to the embers of convoluted despair. The water hisses where it meets the tongues of its nemesis. Drops of water rain down on charred bodies, on a car torn in half, on human bodies torn to pieces. The water glides down a solitary human arm lost in this burnt carnage, streams of tears in search of solace.

A man stands amid the massacre. Beads of sweat glisten on his face, growing and conjoining till they slide onto his neck where his burn scar sits. He breathes in the scene before him, desolate questions choking in the air he breathes out. All around him, there are cries of anguish from those with parts of their bodies blown off, those with their skin blackened, those searching for family or friend, those who have found family or friend. Charred. Killed.

He searches desperately for her. He sees a woman lying face down on the street. He heaves at her body, turning her over. It is not her. He breathes a small sigh of relief. He goes to another body. He stops breathing. He turns the body. He breathes again.

He hears the cries again, the excruciating voice of pain emanating from the hospital bed a long time ago, encapsulating the unspeakable anguish of the body embracing a raw wound in the aftermath of its skin being burned. Tears seeped into his eyes, as the penetrating sounds of human helplessness stretched out and embraced him.

He sees the flames again, the colossal yellow tsunami from forty-one years ago which altered their lives, and that of their families, forever. The heat seared into his eyes when, as a boy, he stood for the last time outside his attap house, gazing in awe at the spectacular leaps of burning sun.

He feels again the touch of her hand, her lips, her body, soft and warm in its caress, yet bold and unflinching in bearing his brokenness. He hears her voice calling him, *Yang.*

Snow, where are you? He is unable to find her. Have their lives, everything that they have been through, come to this?

As he beholds the ruins, tears once more burn his eyes. Splinters of pain swirl in vague, undefinable inner chambers. His stomach clenches into a fist—a helpless, cornered fist which, unable to hit out in anger at another, can only punch inward, effecting what pain it can with each strike, till he is brought down on one knee.

The wound on his leg, just above the bent knee, continues to bleed.

Chapter 2

The scar sits unapologetic where the skin was once smooth and supple. A flaw in humanity's evolution. Severely damaged skin can heal, but it cannot regenerate. Instead, it forms scars—tissue that seems thicker but is, in fact, weaker.

Evolution has selected speed over perfection. In healthy skin, collagen fibres form a lattice. But as wounds heal, collagen fibres are laid down parallel, creating tissue that is stiff and weak. Not having sweat glands, the scar tissue is dry and itchy. It prevents the body from cooling off.

The skin will never be the way it was before. Unable to return to its original state. It will need to be tended to with constant care. It will stare impassively at those who look upon its bearer with disbelief or disgust.

Has the wound healed where the scar sits?

In some ways, it surely has. The wound has closed, no longer permitting the admittance of microbial enemies which endanger the entire body. Where the wound had once been the source of pain, the scar lies inert.

Yet, perhaps, the scar will always be a symbol of something changed, of a wound that has healed, but not completely. Never completely. We must henceforth pay heed to our scars.

How do we walk on, bearing these scars?
Perhaps that is a question life throws at each one of us.

Part One

Fire

Light and life gifted by the sun
Yet scars are overflowing

***

1961
Singapore

Chapter 3

Singapore, 1961.

A thousand resplendent arrows of soft fire shot through the sky, gliding, and lodging themselves in the sea of attap; splinters of light from an awakening sun. A tiny sunbird flitted about, sprightly in its olive green and bright yellow. The morning breeze stroked the dunes of attap rising and falling ceaselessly; wind which brought with it the sweet scent of the morning dew together with the sour stench of the rubbish in the clogged drains and the faecal waste of humans and animals alike.

Six-year-old Yang sat up on his mat. He rubbed his eyes; then looked around absent-mindedly. The chickens pecked at the muddy ground, one of them nibbling from a heap of rotting vegetables in the nearby *longkang*, the small drain in front of their hut. A hen came bobbing near his feet, searching for earthworms. *Ah yes*, now he remembered—he had carried his mat out of his attap house last night; it was cooler to sleep outside in this hot, humid April weather.

All around him, in the adjacent attap houses, wood fires were being kindled by his neighbours who, like his family, lived behind Beo Lane in their kampong, Bukit Ho Swee. Pots and pans clanked as breakfast was made. Babies cried, adults called out to their children, people gargled as they brushed their teeth. He inhaled the aroma of *you tiao*—the dough fritters—being fried in woks of oil above crackling wood fires; fires which exhaled smoke along with their bountiful heat, heat that would soon provide nourishment for all.

In the kitchen of his small attap house, Dai Kah Jie (elder sister) and Yee Kah Jie (second sister) hummed as they helped Ma prepare the pot of peanut porridge which he would soon have to help sell.

'Lee Yang! Wake up!' came Ma's shrill voice.

He stood up; rolled up his mat. He scampered past the rows of haphazardly built wooden houses towards the wooden shed shared by his family and their neighbours. Perhaps the heavens were smiling on him this morning, granting his wish for a short queue. Within five minutes he was squatting over the pail, relieving himself.

A familiar snort. Ah Poop, the pig whose pigsty was built beside the communal toilet, greeted him. A trapdoor had been made for the free-range pigs to go for the human waste, rendering toilet encounters with the pigs frequent. He had named this pig Ah Poop, for it ate his poop every day.

'Hello Ah Poop!'

Snort.

'Okay, okay. Going to finish. Wait ah!'

Snort.

'Aiya, why I take so long? Stomachache lah!'

He wiped his backside with newspaper, pulled up his shorts, then ran back to the small vegetable patch outside his hut, where he plucked a partially rotten brinjal. Dashing back to the pigsty, he threw the vegetable to his pig-friend.

Knowing he would be in trouble if he tarried any longer, he hurried back to his house. As he neared the door, he could hear Ma grumbling, 'Where is that boy? Always running around when I need him to carry the porridge!' Her voice increased in volume till, finally, he heard the shriek he had grown accustomed to, 'Lee Yang! Where are you?'

'I'm here!' he shouted.

The building with the word 'Pepsi' finally came into view. Not having started school, he had yet to learn how to read, but he recognized the word 'Pepsi' as the place where bottles of sweet, brown drinks were made; the place where Ba—his father– worked as a deliveryman.

Having pushed their food cart with the pot of porridge all the way from their home to the Pepsi factory at Havelock Road, he pulled at the sweat-soaked shirt stuck to his back. Worse than the physical exertion of the journey, which took them almost an hour, was Ma's constant nagging and grumbling.

'Every day you and your sisters give me a headache and a backache! Why must my life be so full of toil? Life is so unkind to me! Better not to have you and your sisters. My cousin is so lucky. Her husband owns a provision shop in Ipoh, and every day, she just sits in the shop and earns money. No need to slog like me,' she ranted in Cantonese. '*San fu ah, San fu!* Hard life, hard life!'

He wanted to remind her that his sisters were at home, helping with the cooking and cleaning, that he was pushing the cart for her, but he remembered the stern rebuke he had received when he had tried to say so last week—*of course, all of you should be helping!* she had berated him—so he held his tongue and continued pushing.

Her energies were, at last, diverted towards getting the factory workers to patronize their makeshift stall beside the Pepsi building. 'Delicious porridge! Come and try!' she called out. Looking attractive in her peach-coloured floral samfoo, she smiled coyly at the men passing by. She had large eyes and luscious lips—a pretty woman, one could say—and some of the men, smiling back, came over. Yang served the porridge to those who sought the comfort of warm broth or the presence of a warm woman. A man asked Ma for her name. With a coquettish laugh, she replied, 'I'm Tan Ah Feng. Call me Ah Feng. It means Phoenix, I'm sure you know!'

Yang saw Ba drive the delivery truck out of the factory. On some days, the drinks had to be delivered to the Central Area surrounding the Singapore River, on others to the shops in the surrounding kampongs.

After the porridge had been sold, Yang and Ma made their way back. Nearing their kampong, they saw Ba's lorry parked close to some of the kampong's shops. Ma stopped abruptly in her tracks. Craning her neck to locate her husband, she frowned when she saw him in Tan's Provision Shop, owned by the family of an Indonesian-Chinese neighbour whom the kampong folk affectionately called Nenek, meaning Grandma.

'Yang,' Ma commanded in a hushed voice, 'Go and see what your Ba is doing in the shop. Don't say I asked you to go, and don't say I'm here. Understand? Go!'

Wanting to ask why she did not want to go and see for herself, but not wanting to be admonished for questioning her orders, he obeyed. He entered the provision shop.

Nenek's daughter-in-law, Aunty Su Mei, or Mei Ah-Yee as the children called her, was at the counter. She smiled at Yang when he walked in. Ba was in the middle isle, bent at the waist as he unloaded the bottles of Pepsi, arranging them on a shelf. He caught sight of his son and straightened.

'What are you doing here?' he asked, his voice detached, his face impassive.

Ma's instructions ran through Yang's mind. He was to watch what Ba was doing but was not to say that Ma had sent him here and that she was outside. It struck him at this moment that Ma had sent him here to be a spy. The thought sent tingles of thrill through his sunbaked, skinny frame, but he did not know how to reply to his Ba's question.

He stood there, eyes wide and mouth agape. He scoured his memory for what his best friend Ah Pui, meaning Fatty, had told him about being a spy when they had played games of spy and thief. Ah Pui knew a lot of things because he read lots of comics, and he had said that spies had to pretend. Watch your target but pretend not to watch.

But he still did not know how to answer Ba's question. An impatient look spread across Ba's face. Perhaps the heavens were still smiling on him, an innocent spy carrying out his duty, for Mei Ah-Yee called him over to the counter. Pulling out a lollipop in pink wrapper—cola-flavoured, his favourite—she held it out to him. He took it eagerly, as he mumbled a 'thank you'.

Ba continued to place the Pepsi bottles on the shelf. Relieved that he had been let off the hook, Yang sauntered around the shop. *Watch your target but pretend not to watch.* He wondered how long he was supposed to spy on Ba, and what Ma was expecting him to spy on. The lollipop was already in his tummy, and he was getting so bored, he began to whistle. He soon realized that this was a bad idea when his whistling caught Ba's attention once again. So, when Nenek walked in, he ran to greet her.

Nenek was carrying her one-year-old granddaughter, whom she put down as she addressed Yang, 'Yang! Help Nenek keep an eye on Xue'er, okay?'

Ba came over, collected the payment for the drinks he had delivered, and walked out, telling Yang as he left, 'Don't get into trouble.'

Yang stared at the little girl sitting on the floor. She was strumming her lips with her fingers, blowing bubbles of saliva into them. He sat down in front of her. Wasn't that what Nenek had asked him to do, to keep an eye on her? He thought to himself that he liked her name, Xue'er. Little Snow. Little did he know that, like Snow, she would completely transform the landscape of his life in time to come.

Little Snow looked at him. Without warning, she reached out, grabbed a tuft of his hair, and pulled hard.

'Ow! Ow! Lemme go! Lemme go!' he screeched. He squirmed, tried to twist his body so she would let go, but she would not release her grip. Instead, she started giggling as he writhed in agony. Nenek and Mei Ah-Yee, who were poring over a book, looked up. They, too, started laughing.

He grabbed her hand and yanked hard. Finally, his hair was free. He dashed out of the shop, regretting that he had liked her name, and swearing never to go near her again.

Outside, Ma was no longer where she had been when he had entered the shop. He ran around, looking for her, eventually spotting her hiding behind a wall. She must have gone undercover when Ba had come out of the shop.

A cheeky smile spread across his face, the opportunity of playing a prank on Ma too irresistible a lure. Covering his mouth to stifle his chuckles, he tiptoed, crept up behind her, and with a loud 'boo!' he leapt out, landing at her side with peals of laughter.

She jumped up with a shriek, swivelling around with her hand on her chest. When she saw him, her face scrunched up, and before he could run, she grabbed him by the ear, twisting forcefully as he yelped in pain. Still pinching his ear, she asked him what he had seen in the shop. 'Nothing,' he replied, grimacing. She seemed relieved, finally releasing his ear, but the next minute her admonishment resumed. 'Take so long inside and now you say nothing! You made me wait so long outside, do you know? All for nothing! Useless, all of you!'

On and on she went as they made their way home, with him rubbing his throbbing ear and his head where his hair had been yanked.

Chapter 4

The sounds of humble human fellowship swayed in the open space beside the rows of attap houses in the night; the kampong children laughed and played, Yang amongst them; the womenfolk chatted, bemoaning their laborious daily lives, of mouths to feed and ends to meet; of muscles sore from cooking and cleaning; of skin scalded from globules of jumping hot oil; of fingers cramped from sewing all day, weaving clothing to supplement the family income.

Nearby, in a kampong coffee shop, the menfolk—Yang's Ba among them—lit their cigarettes and licked the froth on their lips, remnants of beer washed down all too soon; gave their two cents worth of whether their country ought to merge with their larger northern neighbour, and melded into a collective masculine companionship as the night wore on.

The darkened sky proffered its generosity of a thousand smiling stars—a companionship of sorts to the lonely, earthly souls below. Outside the attap huts, the children fell into a hushed silence as an old grandmother, pointing to the stars above, began regaling them with the legend of the cowherd and the weaving maiden:

The cowherd stood on the riverbank, gazing at the heavenly maiden bathing in the stream. Her long, silky hair draped her shoulders as she raised her slender arms, pouring the cool water over her head.

The heavenly maiden, whose duty it was to weave the clothing of the gods, had descended to earth with her six sisters. The cowherd asked his magic cow if he should steal her clothes, for then the lovely goddess might marry him. Looking at its master, the cow opened its mouth to speak.

The cowherd stole the maiden's clothes and she married him. However, as she neglected her weaving duties, she was summoned back to the heavens. The cowherd was heartbroken. The cow sacrificed itself so its master could ascend the heavens on its hide to meet the goddess. The gods were furious at their reunion. They turned the lovers into stars, separated by the Milky Way.

Later, the god of heaven, moved by their love and taking pity on them, allowed them to meet once a year, on the seventh day of the seventh lunar month.

'Ohh, why does it have such a sad ending?' Yee Kah Jie sighed.

'Serves him right for stealing her clothes,' Dai Kah Jie remarked, looking miffed.

Yee Kah Jie was more sympathetic. 'If a man could fall so madly in love with me, I would gladly marry him,' she said dreamily.

'He's only a cowherd, poor, and with no future,' Dai Kah Jie retorted.

'But in our kampong, there are no cows! We only have chickens and ducks and pigs!' one of the children exclaimed.

'Ya,' another chimed in, 'Is a chickenherd the same as a cowherd? *Ji Lang* instead of *Niu Lang*?'

'Yes, yes!' the children started to giggle. A hand shot up. 'I will be *Zhu Lang*, pigherd!' Another young boy said eagerly, 'I will be *Ya Lang*, duckherd!' He pointed at Yang and said, 'Yang, you can be *Ji Lang*, chickenherd!'

Yang thought of his chickens. He imagined the heavenly maiden in the stream; wondered if she became like his mother after she married the cowherd. He remembered the little girl in the provision shop, Little Snow. Was it possible for a little girl blowing bubbles with her saliva to become a heavenly maiden bathing in the stream? He wondered.

The next day, Yang went with Ah Pui and Alif, a Malay neighbour, to a disused cemetery atop the hill to play and dig for bones, as they often did. The mud flew in the air as they thrust their wooden sticks into the ground.

'Psst! Yang, Alif, over here!' Ah Pui called out.

Yang and Alif scampered over to where Ah Pui had dug a hole. They peered in. True enough, an ivory-coloured solid peered back at them from the ground below. The three boys flung aside their sticks, started digging with their bare hands, exhilarated at their find.

Suddenly, Ah Pui groaned and plonked onto the ground, lying flat on his back. For an instant he did not move, but soon his fat tummy began wobbling in his T-shirt as he tried to stifle a giggle. Yang and Alif looked from Ah Pui to one another and chuckled.

'Alif, looks like Ah Pui is dead!' Yang said as loudly as he could.

'Alamak! We better bury him!' Alif replied.

They grabbed Ah Pui by the legs; he started kicking and they chased one another down the hill.

They were panting when they reached the coffee shop owned by Ah Pui's family, one of the better off families in the kampong. They had a large, well-ventilated wooden house, unlike Yang's small, dingy attap house. Ah Pui had good food to eat and comics to read.

Yang and Alif revelled in their friend's material abundance as they sat in the coffee shop, slurping refreshing cups of iced milo, and sharing a plate of piping hot *char kway teow*. Sitting at the table next to theirs were two tall young men whom some people called *pai kia*, meaning bad kids in Hokkien. They were the kampong gangsters, though Ah Pui said that they were not really bad, that they were often brave and righteous, protecting the kampong from intrusion by other gangs.

Yang cast a sidelong glance at the two men. One of them noticed it. Giving Yang a wink, he gestured with his hand for him to move closer. Gingerly, Yang complied.

'I'm Chen Long. People call me Ah Long, like the dragon. You can call me Long Kor.'

'Long Kor,' Yang greeted Big Brother Dragon.

'What's your name?'

'Yang. Lee Yang.'

'Which 'Yang'?'

'The sun.'

'Hmm, Yang. Like the sun. Sun means fire. I'm the dragon, you're the fire. We go hand in hand, you know?' Long Kor winked at him again, as he shook his hand.

For the first time in his life, Yang felt like a man. He felt as though, like the dragon and the fire, he could be strong, powerful, and brave.

In the mundane, old coffee shop, the fire of a friendship was born, one that would steer the course of Yang's growing years.

As he approached his house that evening, Yang could hear Ma's voice from afar, nagging at Ba, or Dai Kah Jie, or Yee Kah Jie. He slipped in quietly through the door.

'Day in and day out, I have to slog and slog,' Ma grumbled to Ba, without looking at him, as she stirred the porridge on the stove. 'Why can't you get a better job? Go and work in the town. Maybe you can earn more there! Ah Yang starts primary school next year, and we have to buy books and school uniforms! My cousin in Ipoh is so lucky. Her husband owns a provision shop, and all she has to do is sit there and collect money. What about me? What have you given me?'

The muscles in Ba's jaw tensed as he pulled off his wet shirt, soaked with perspiration after a day of deliveries. Yang looked at Ba's strong, muscular shoulders with admiration. Dai Kah Jie scooped a bowl of porridge, placing it on the table for Ba, but Ba pulled on a clean shirt, took his pack of cigarettes, and walked out of the house.

Ba's withdrawals had become more frequent of late. Usually, Yang would scoop his own porridge and sit down to eat. This evening he decided to follow Ba outside.

Ba sat on a wooden plank outside the house, taking long, hard pulls at his cigarette. Gingerly, Yang went to sit beside him. Ba glanced briefly at him, then went back to his own thoughts without saying a word.

Sudden pangs of guilt stabbed at Yang. Did Ma and Ba's unhappiness have something to do with his spying in the provision shop? Was Ba angry with him for helping Ma spy on him? He wanted to ask Ba if he was angry. He wanted to ask Ba why he hardly spoke to Ma, hardly spoke to his sisters, hardly spoke to him. Had he, or Dai Kah Jie, or Yee Kah Jie, done something wrong? Yet, as he sat there beside his Ba, he could not ask; did not dare to ask.

He rubbed one foot against the other, watching the dirt fall to the ground as he and Ba sat there in silence. Then, Ba stubbed out his cigarette, said to him, 'Go back,' and walked off.

Later that night, when all of them had gone to bed, Yang heard Ba come home as he lay half asleep. Ba tripped over him— for he slept on his mat near the doorway—and he thought Ba reeked of beer.

Father and son soon fell asleep, finding rest in oblivion; a blissful slumber shared with half the earth's inhabitants; an oft-forgotten uncertainty hovering above lives so helpless, and so hopeful.

Chapter 5

All it took was tinder. A spark, a little fire used for cooking perhaps, and a sea of tinder-dry attap. A haughty sun, breathing his rhythms of light and heat. An occasional gust of arid wind. As was the way of disasters, it arrived unexpectedly on this afternoon in May. The day which would render sixteen thousand people homeless began like any other day.

Outside the family hut, Yang herded his family's chickens towards the vegetable patch, then back towards the hut. He threw them a handful of leftover rice. He watched them listlessly. Ba had left the house in the morning of this Hari Raya Haji public holiday, while his sisters had gone with Ma to visit a relative, leaving him alone at home.

Sudden shouts rang out from the houses near the edge of the kampong. He looked in that direction. Thick plumes of black smoke were rising in the air above the neighbouring kampong. He gasped.

Shouts of 'Fire! Fire!' became louder, more urgent. He stood up but did not know what to do. The black smoke seemed to be getting closer. Some of the neighbours started grabbing their belongings and running; others shouted to one another, 'Run! Quickly run!'

Yang gazed in awe at the fire in the distance and, for a moment, thought that it was the most magnificent thing he had ever seen. In a way he could not understand (was it because he was named after the mighty sun?) he felt as if the fire was his friend.

'Yang! Grab your things quickly and run! There's a big fire coming our way!' Uncle Lim, a neighbour, yelled when he saw Yang standing stupefied. Yang nodded frantically. He dashed into his house. But what should he grab? Should he grab their clothes? The old rice-cooker? Or Ma's sewing machine? Once again, he was at a loss. How was he going to find his Ba, Ma, and sisters?

He darted outside to check on the fire's advance. Now people were screaming and running helter-skelter along the narrow lanes, carrying or dragging bags of belongings, scurrying away from the fast-approaching flames.

An old man and woman were pushing a cartful of chairs, pots, and pans. A mother carrying a baby in her arms was fleeing with three other children holding on to her samfoo— one gripping the fabric on her left, another to her right, and the third one behind. She scuttled along with her children in tow, then stopped abruptly, disoriented, looking this way and that, before hurrying away in a different direction, all the while with frenzied, tearful commands to her young ones to hold on to her tightly.

Up in the air some distance away, the wind carried with it a torched piece of zinc roofing—a blazing, incandescent kite— only to drop it nonchalantly onto an attap house across the lane. The attap burst into flames. The fiery tongues licked and devoured the adjacent attap houses before one could blink an eye.

For the first time since he saw the smoke, Yang felt alone; felt afraid. The heat swept in like invisible, violent waves upon a shore in a storm, searing into his eyes, smarting them in a way he had never experienced before.

He swivelled to gape at the blaze, then back at his house. Grabbing two chickens, one in each arm, he began running like everyone else. He bumped into others, just as they bumped into him, his heart racing wildly through the squall of shouts and screams and tears.

Run! Run! he kept telling himself as he cast occasional glances backward at the colossal, majestic flames. Panting, he reached the end of the lane along which his house had been built.

Then, much to his relief, he caught sight of Ma, Dai Kah Jie, and Yee Kah Jie. Strangely though, they were running headlong into the retreating throngs of people.

'Ma, Dai Kah Jie, Yee Kah Jie! Fire! Fire! Everyone is running away!'

'Yah, we know! We saw the fire!' Da Kah Jie shouted above the din. 'Ma wanted to come back to get her sewing machine!'

Ma saw the two chickens Yang was carrying and hollered, 'Stupid boy! Take the chickens for what!'

'Ma, never mind the sewing machine. Don't go, it's dangerous!' Yee Kah Jie cried.

'Do you know how much the sewing machine costs? Dai Kah Jie, take care of your sister and brother! I'll look for you later!'

With that, Ma ran back towards their house.

Yee Kah Jie stood there, sobbing. Grabbing her with one hand and Yang with the other, Dai Kah Jie pulled them along the lane. When they came to Havelock Road, however, the crowd began to disperse in all directions, and they did not know which way to go.

As they stood there, two fire engines arrived and, with them, dozens of firefighters. In their fire suits, they began directing jets of water at the blaze. Just as they seemed to be making headway though, more tongues of fire roared against them. Their leader had to shout his instructions to his men, telling them that the blaze was too large, that he would have to call for reinforcements.

'Yang!' came a shout.

Yang turned around.

'Long Kor!' he called out, his spirits lifted by the appearance of his friend, Big Brother Dragon. Long Kor must have seen them standing there on the road amidst the throng, disoriented.

'I saw policemen directing people this way. Come on!' Long Kor hastened towards the right, beckoning Yang and his sisters to follow. After a while he told them to keep going. 'I'm going back to see if anyone else needs help!' he exclaimed as he turned and sprinted back towards the kampong.

They moved along with the crowd, Yang clutching their chickens which repeatedly tried to flap their wings, as if sensing the panic and chaos around them. Even as they retreated, they could feel the heat from the inferno pushing them forward relentlessly. When Yang turned back to look, all he could see of his kampong were their burning houses coughing out thick, black smoke.

An elderly man carrying a small table on his shoulders cried out, '*Lao tian ah lao tian*, dear old heavens, why is this happening? We have homes no more. We are homeless now!'

Yee Kah Jie stuttered between sobs, 'Ma …Ma …' Dai Kah Jie tried to reassure them, 'Ma will know what to do.'

The sky had darkened by the time they arrived at River Valley Primary School. Hundreds of fire victims were already in the school compound; hundreds more were surging in. Yang and his sisters were directed by the police and government officials to a classroom on the third storey of the school building.

The three siblings and their two chickens huddled in a corner of the classroom that night, dozing off intermittently, hopeful that Ma and Ba would find them there in the morning, with a heaviness sinking into their hearts along with the descent of the night.

Chapter 6

Yang woke up to the wails of a baby whose family occupied another corner of the classroom. Adults were handing biscuits to their children for breakfast. A rumbling came from his stomach. He swallowed; he and his sisters had not had anything to eat since their escape from the fire.

Yee Kah Jie walked into the room with a mug of water in one hand and biscuits in the other. Yang gulped down the water, then stuffed his mouth with the biscuits ravenously.

'Where's Dai Kah Jie?' he asked, his mouth still full of biscuit.

'She went to register for us. All the fire victims have to register. Then, maybe,' she paused, fear and uncertainty glazing her eyes, 'Ba and Ma can find us.'

He was about to gobble down the last two biscuits, but the sad, lost look on Yee Kah Jie's face made him shove the biscuits into her hand. 'Give you. They're delicious,' he told her.

A few men in the room were discussing loudly the cause of the fire. 'It started in Kampong Tiong Bahru lah. A cooking fire there made the attap roof catch fire. Then, swoosh!' one man exclaimed. An old man added, 'I've never seen such a big fire in my life!'

Just then, Dai Kah Jie came in all excited. 'Ba found us! Ba found us! He saw me outside and told us to stay here. He's going to look for Ma.' Dai Kah Jie had more water and biscuits. The three of them relished it as though it were the best meal they had ever eaten.

Later that morning, blankets and mattresses were distributed to them, supplied by the British Army. Meals were provided by the government. Loudspeakers blared through the day, with messages and instructions in English, Mandarin, Hokkien, Cantonese, and Teochew. From the parapet on the third storey, they saw the prime minister, Mr Lee Kuan Yew, who was visiting the fire victims at the schools which housed them.

In the afternoon, the adults in the classroom—which was now their home for the time being—were talking about an elderly man and woman who had perished in the conflagration. Yang and his sisters listened, as blood drained off their faces, wondering if Ma had managed to escape.

Ba strode in.

'Ma had some burns and is in the hospital, but she's okay,' Ba told them. He went on, 'I'm going to the fire site, to see if ...' Ba did not finish his sentence. Yang asked to go along.

They made their way to the fire site. It was cordoned off, with police officers and soldiers standing guard at the entrances. Clouds of smoke still hung over the area, along with the fetid smell of burnt animal carcasses, zinc roofing, chemicals from the factories, furniture, and all other items which had defined their daily existence. They stepped across charred wood and furniture as they made their way to the place which was once their home.

Yang ran ahead of Ba towards the wooden shed where he had peed and pooped each day. He heaved at a burnt piece of wood, pushing it aside. He came face-to-face with a completely blackened carcass of a pig.

'Ah Poop,' he whispered, head bowed, shoulders drooping.

He stood there, repulsed by the grotesque sight and putrid stench, yet pulled to linger on by memories of his animal-friend.

Ba was staring at the burnt attap house they used to call home. Some of their neighbours were there too, searching for their belongings beneath the collapsed wood and zinc, some sighing or weeping, others shaking their heads. Darker than the smoke and heavier than the stench was the smothering despondency that hung in the air; the tears, sighs, and hopelessness of sixteen thousand homeless people bearing down on the ashes.

Ba's face was sullen. Yang came over and stood beside him. Uncle Lim, their neighbour, was standing there as well. He turned to look at Ba, his eyes watery.

'Kim Fatt, everything is gone. Nothing left. What do we do now? What's going to happen to us?'

In a hoarse, hollow voice Yang had never heard before, Ba replied without looking at anyone, 'I don't know.' The muscles in his neck tightened, as if he were clenching his jaw. Then his shoulders drooped, and he closed his eyes.

Yang had never been to a hospital before. He stared, bewildered, at the people lying on the beds: some with bandages around their arms or legs, others with tubes sticking out of their bodies; some asleep, others groaning in pain. The smell of sickness and medicine made him pinch his nose.

'Come on, we've to go see Ma,' Dai Kah Jie pulled him along. With his nose still pinched, he walked with Dai Kah Jie behind Ba and Yee Kah Jie into the ward at the General Hospital.

Ma was propped up on a bed, with bandages stuck to her left cheek and neck. When she saw them, she snapped at him, 'Why are you pinching your nose? Am I very smelly?' He immediately put his hand down.

Yee Kah Jie asked timidly, 'Ma, did your face get burned? Will there be a scar?'

Ma seemed to fly into a rage at Yee Kah Jie's question, snarling, 'I look very ugly now, is it? It's because of all of you! I wouldn't have gone back if not for all of you!'

Yee Kah Jie averted her eyes as she tried to stifle her sobs.

'You should not have gone back,' Ba said, his face expressionless.

Ma glared at him, mouthing her words slowly, 'I would not have gone back if you had been with us.'

Ba's breathing quickened and loudened. 'I was out looking for jobs,' he said with effort, the words ratcheted forward by a cauldron of fury simmering just below the surface.

Yang looked from his Ma to his Ba, sensing but not understanding the undertones of anger in their words and stares. Fortunately, two nurses came over, telling them that they had to change Ma's dressing.

One of them smiled kindly as she explained, 'It can be very painful when we change dressings for burn patients, because it is very raw where the burnt skin had to be removed. But there is no choice. We have to change the dressing to keep the wound clean, to prevent infection. Your wife only suffered minor burns to a small area on her face and neck, so it shouldn't be too painful.'

Ba nodded. The nurses pulled the curtain around Ma's bed. Yang and his family stood waiting along the corridor. As the nurses changed Ma's dressing, her shrieks and cries of pain could be heard from behind the curtain. 'Stop! Ow, ow!

Hou tong ah, very painful! No, stop!' Her shrieks stopped after a few minutes; presumably the task was accomplished.

Yang saw Nenek at the other end of the ward, carrying her granddaughter, the girl who had pulled his hair and whose name he still remembered. Little Snow. A man whom he recognized as Little Snow's father was standing beside them. Two nurses now pulled the curtains around the bed where they were standing, in the same way his Ma had the curtains drawn. The one on the hospital bed must be Aunty Su Mei, Little Snow's mother.

He wandered closer to them; they did not notice him, for a doctor was speaking to them. The doctor, looking apologetic, said something about not being able to save her eyes, and that her face was badly burned. Nenek wiped the tears from her eyes; her son stared at the floor. Little Snow was hugging her Nenek, resting her head on the old woman's shoulder.

There came anguished cries from within the drawn curtains. They were not cries of anger, but rather of excruciating pain which seemed many times more than his Ma's. The cries reverberated in his head, boring into him an epiphany of what the fire really meant, awakening in him a sensation—an undefinable discomfort which began when he saw Ah Poop's burnt body and when he stood with Ba staring at their burnt house—of the darkness that fire could beget. When he lifted his hand to rub his eyes, there was a residue of moisture on his fingers he could not explain.

There came a sudden tug on his arm, along with the hushed, urgent voice of Dai Kah Jie. 'Ba's leaving. Let's go!' He went along, not understanding why Ba was leaving so abruptly.

Near the relief centre, Yang saw from a distance a fat boy jumping up and down outside the fence, as if trying to catch a glimpse of something or someone inside, his tummy wobbling inside his T-shirt with each jump.

'Ah Pui! Ah Pui!' he yelled, elated as he ran towards his best friend.

'Yang! I've been looking for you!'

'Me too!'

The two boys stood facing each other, panting—one from running and the other from jumping—while Ah Pui scratched his head awkwardly. Unlike his friend, Yang was scrawny, and the duo got along like Laurel and Hardy.

'Was your house, your coffee shop, burnt down by the fire?' Yang asked.

'Ya,' Ah Pui nodded and sighed, 'it was destroyed. Your house too?'

Yang nodded. 'Where have you been staying?'

'I'm staying with my uncle. He has a house and a coffee shop in Kallang. Block 15. You? Where is your family going to live?'

Yang shrugged, looking down momentarily. 'I don't know.'

'You can come and look for me in Kallang. I have to go now. My Ma's waiting for me.'

They were about to part ways when Yang remembered something. He blurted out, 'Wait, I'll be back in a minute!' and sprinted back inside the school. When he came out a minute later, he was carrying his two chickens.

'I grabbed our chickens before running. But now I don't know what's going to happen to my family. Whether or not we will have a house to live in,' he paused, looking down again before shoving the chickens towards Ah Pui. 'Here, give them to you. They're good chickens, gave us lots of eggs. You can sell their half-boiled eggs in your coffee shop!'

Ah Pui took hold of the hens, not knowing what to say. 'Okay,' he finally said. He turned to go, then stopped after a few steps and turned back to wave goodbye to his friend. 'Remember, okay? Kallang, Block 15!'

Yang looked on as Ah Pui's figure became smaller and smaller till it disappeared into the distance, wondering if he would ever see his friend again.

Life went on at the relief centre. Meals were provided to the thousands of homeless fire victims who slept on mattresses in the classrooms. They queued to collect water at standpipes, where they also washed their laundry and where mothers bathed their young children who stood there in their shorts and knickers. There was even a haircut day—termed 'Operation Haircut' in the newspapers—during which dozens of barbers from the Singapore Barbers' Association volunteered their services, pro bono, to the fire victims.

The schools were not designed to accommodate such large numbers of people though. Congestion led to poor hygiene, what with thrown away food and rubbish choking the drains, and cases of measles and dysentery started developing.

One morning, Ba told Yang and his sisters that they would be moving to a temporary house in Kallang. They overheard the adults lamenting about the rent they would have to pay for rental flats, which ranged from $20 a month for a one-room flat to $80 for a three-room flat, causing much anxiety. As usual, Ba did not say anything to Yang and his sisters, though he frowned and smoked a lot more than he normally did.

On 4 June, ten days after the conflagration, along with thousands of other fire victims, Yang and his family boarded army lorries bound for one- and two-room flats in government housing estates in Kallang and other parts of the country.

Chapter 7

Their new home was a queer place.

The most fascinating part was the magic box into which you could enter, only to be miraculously transported to a different place with the press of a button. From down on the earth to up in the sky—for they now lived up in the sky—like earthlings rising heavenward. But it worked the other way round too. From up in the sky to down on the earth. Heavenly beings falling back to the earth. Up and down, heaven and earth; earthly beings rising and falling, rising and falling—this happened to everyone, every day.

Then there was the magic hole into which their pee and their poop could disappear when they pulled a string with a plastic handle. Yang thought of Ah Poop, his pig-friend who had happily awaited his poop-breakfast each morning. What would Ah Poop have for breakfast now, if he had still been alive?

His new home up in the sky, with its grey walls and small windows, was no magic house though. The one-room flat was much smaller than their attap house in the kampong. The most frustrating part was not being able to carry his mattress outside, where it was cooler, to sleep at night. Like the classroom at the relief centre, once you stepped outside, you entered the common corridor, where other people walked to get to and from their own flats.

Ba, too, did not seem to like being in the flat much, though he said nothing. He resumed his job as a delivery man, spending the after-work hours leaning on the parapet outside, brooding and smoking, or going to a coffee shop nearby. He spent part of their rehabilitation allowance buying second-hand utensils, a small table with four rickety stools, and some clothes for them. Yang whiled the time away at Ah Pui's coffee shop, which he found after some searching.

A week after moving into their new home, Ba went to the hospital to bring Ma home. Yang and his sisters waited in their flat, eager and relieved that their mother would soon be home, yet with no small amount of dread and trepidation.

When a sullen Ma and Ba stepped into the house, Yang did not know what to do. Dai Kah Jie had instructed them not to say anything, lest it triggered a tirade from Ma. While he and his sisters were somewhat accustomed to her constant criticisms and lamentations, there was now an anger which could be ignited by the smallest spark, perhaps not dissimilar to their attap houses bursting into flames when a piece of zinc roofing was blown onto them by a guiltless wind.

Yang took his cue from his sisters, helping Ma take her bag without saying a word. She was wearing a scarf around her head which covered her left cheek, where the bandage had been. Without taking off her scarf, Ma looked around the small room that was now their home. She sat down on one of the stools, looking blankly ahead, still not saying anything.

'Ma, I'll show you where the bathroom and toilet are,' Yee Kah Jie offered apprehensively. Ma stood up and followed her.

Ba was outside smoking again. Yang busied himself helping Dai Kah Jie prepare dinner. Yee Kah Jie handed Ma a towel and some clean clothes, which Ma took, still not uttering a word. She stood there for a moment, looking at no one. Finally, her breathing becoming heavier, she pulled the scarf off.

Dai kah Jie and Yee Kah Jie gasped, but quickly looked away when Ma looked daggers at them.

Stretching from her lower cheek down to her neck was a swollen, reddish scar the size of a small kitchen knife.

Chapter 8

Ah Feng stared at the oval, handheld mirror the size of a frying pan, the one she had asked her husband to buy for her. She ran her fingers across the smooth skin on her right cheek, scrutinizing the unblemished image on the mirror which seemed to sparkle with the brushes of the morning light. Her muscles tensing, she turned her face slowly toward the right, watching as the bulging red blotch edged into sight, staring back at her with a mocking vengeance. She slapped the mirror face down onto the table, tears burning her eyes.

Yang looked up at the sound of the mirror's loud flap on the table. He was seated on the floor in their flat, flicking his marbles about. Dai Kah Jie and Yee Kah Jie had gone to the market, while Ba was packing his clothes into a bag.

'Am I, now, too ugly for you? Is that why you want to leave?' Ma blurted out without looking at Ba.

'Haven't I told you already? Now we have to pay $20 rent every month. I found a job in the Central Area. Isn't that what you always wanted?'

Ma did not say anything. Ba continued, 'And this flat is too small for all of us. So, I'm going to share a room with the friend who helped me find this job. I'll come on Sundays.'

'Who is this lousy friend of yours who makes you leave your family? Is your friend a man or a woman?'

'*Lam yarn*, a man. Okay? And he is helping us, so stop calling him a lousy friend!' Ba heaved loudly, apoplectic.

'Why can't you stay here and take a bus to the Central Area to work?' Ma glanced momentarily at Ba, her tone now softened, her eyes like that of a child pleading not to be left alone.

Ba sighed and shook his head, the way a tired, vexed parent does. He picked up his bag and turned to look Ma in the eye, not flinching at the scar which was now part of his wife's face.

'You always want everything your way. You wanted me to find a better job, so that's what I did,' he paused, and when he spoke again, there was pain and weariness in his eyes. 'You ask for the sky, and when you get it, you blame others for its weight.'

With that, Ba walked out of the flat. Ma stomped to the kitchen where she stood staring out of the window. Yang, suddenly remembering his game, looked down to find the marbles clenched tightly in his fist, his palms wet with perspiration.

Ba's new job in a carpentry firm enabled the family to pay for monthly rentals and utilities, as well as buy some furniture for their house. He came home on Sundays, as he said he would, though, as had always been the case, spoken exchanges with his wife and children were sparse.

About a year later, they moved yet again, this time to a permanent one-room flat in Bukit Ho Swee, where blocks of Housing and Development Board (HDB) flats had been built by the government to house the fire victims. Their new home was not very different from the flat in Kallang; it was a small space with just enough room for the four of them to roll out their mattresses. Ba continued living with his friend in the Central Area.

The winds of change seemed to blow in torrential gusts—the way of tropical thunderstorms. Together with a new home came a new school life. Ba enrolled Yang and Yee Kah Jie in Kim Seng East School. Dai Kah Jie had to take care of the household chores, the food, and groceries for the family. School would not be a part of her life.

Ma, fearing the stares of others at the scar on her face, hardly stepped out of the house. When she did step out, mostly to go for her hospital check-ups, she would have a scarf around her face. At home, she snapped at her children even more than before, constantly finding fault with Dai Kah Jie's cooking, and berating Yang and Yee Kah Jie for the drain their school fees had on the family's finances. 'It is because of you two that your Ba has to live outside!' she rebuked them.

Yang took to roaming around the estate each afternoon, finding refuge in coffee shops where he was permitted to loiter without having to buy food or drinks. Stepping into a coffee shop one afternoon, he saw a familiar face among a group of burly young men seated at one of the tables. 'Long Kor!' he called out as he approached his friend.

When Long Kor saw him, he broke into a grin, slapped Yang on the back and exclaimed, 'Yo! Ah Yang, my man! Where have you been? A dragon cannot be without fire, you know!'

Yang beamed, feeling the heat of a blush coming to his cheeks at the affirmation of friendship professed by the capable and confident big brother he had come to respect. He was about to recount what had happened after the fire, when the group of young men seated at the adjacent table suddenly overturned their cups.

Some of the people inside and outside the coffee shop started running away from the place, amid shouts of '08 coming! 08 coming!'. One of the stallholders, a kindly man who sold fish ball noodles and with whom Yang had struck up an acquaintance over the months, hurriedly pulled Yang behind his stall, telling him to crouch and be quiet. 'The gangs are fighting for turf,' he whispered. 'The gang known as 24 is fighting its rival gang, the 08.'

From behind the stall, Yang saw a dozen young men fighting one another, some with sticks, others with their bare fists. Long Kor was exchanging punches with a tall, brawny man, who landed a surprise kick on Long Kor's face. Blood oozed from Long Kor's nose as he fell on one knee. Yang's heartbeat accelerated. He grabbed the long metal ladle normally used for scooping out the fish balls and, with a war cry hurtling out from his lungs, ran headlong into the ruckus, lashing out at Long Kor's enemy with all the seven-year-old might he could summon. The enemy ducked; he and his fish ball ladle landed on the ground with a crash and a clank, drawing astonished stares from friend and foe alike.

Long Kor's group of friends started running away. Long Kor pulled Yang up from the ground and shoved him towards the coffee shop before sprinting to join his friends, their rival gang hot on their heels.

Picking up his ladle from the ground, the old, fish-ball seller shook his head, but smiled at Yang. 'You are very brave and righteous, young man. But be careful. Don't play with fire.'

That day, Yang felt as if a fire burned in his chest, the sensation of which lingered long after the sun had quietened, its warmth at once invigorating and sapping, its sound majestic yet menacing, its ebullient energy making him feel courageous, yet fearful.

Yang—like the sun, Long Kor had once said.

There were Sundays when Ba did not come home. At the beginning, such days were few and far between. As time swept the days into weeks and the weeks into months, more and more of Ba's visits seemed to be swept along into the dust as well.

Perhaps Ba found the visits unnecessary. Tiresome even. He had never had much to say to Yang and his sisters, and with Ma, if it wasn't a silence churning with hostility, it was verbal confrontation which was almost always triggered by her tirades and lamentations. Yang did not know whether to look forward to visits from his father, or to dread them. On Saturdays, he and his sisters were on tenterhooks all day; if by noon on Sunday Ba did not show up, they breathed a little easier while bracing themselves for barbed admonishments from Ma.

But Ba did not fail to provide for the family. They were taken care of financially—the rent was never unpaid, food and other necessities were in no short supply, and school fees for Yang and Yee Kah Jie were never in arrears. When he did not visit, he would send money in an envelope or deposit the money in the bank account he had with Ma.

Each day, after school, Yang would either cycle to Kallang— on an old bicycle Ba had given him on one of his visits—to look for Ah Pui, or look up Long Kor at the coffee shops in the vicinity. He hung around with Long Kor, with Long Kor's group of gangsters.

As he grew taller and stronger, so did his kicks and punches; Long Kor taught him how a palm strike should be done, and where you should aim when you kicked (the groin). He went around with Long Kor and his friends, overturned cups in coffee shops to signal a fight, fought for turf alongside his older comrades.

He had to lie to Dai Kah Jie and Yee Kah Jie initially, when they enquired after his whereabouts, but over time, they stopped asking. Ma hardly asked; perhaps she was happier—if a sullen person could be said to be happy—to have him out of her sight. One less bothersome child to rile her.

On his tenth birthday, he counted the weeks Ba had not been home. Twelve weeks. Ba had not visited for three months. Ma's reproaches that Ba had to leave because of him continued to taunt him in his thoughts. He wondered if he now had to become the man of the family.

That was the year his country became independent. Everyone expressed shock and disbelief at the sudden separation from Malaysia.

Uncertainty and apprehension of what lay ahead stared them in the face.

On his eleventh birthday, it became one year and three months since his Ba's last visit. It dawned on him that, perhaps, Ba was not coming back.

Chapter 9

The two teenagers eyed them intently, their hands clenched into fists across their chest, ready to strike or defend, their feet shuffling backwards in small, careful steps. It was quiet in the back alley of Bukit Ho Swee, save for their muffled footfalls and the clattering of plates and pots in some flats above, where the evening meal was being prepared.

Yang and Long Kor had been heading home when they caught sight of the two young men snooping about in the back alley. Long Kor recognized them to be from a rival gang; they had probably been sent to recce the area to aid their gang in turf fights.

They had turned around, startled, when Long Kor shouted 'Don't move!' as he dashed into the alley. They instinctively raised their arms, bracing for attack. The humid air hung heavily around them. One of them wiped away the perspiration on his face with his fist.

'Tell your guys not to intrude on our territory,' Long Kor snarled.

With a shout, one of them—the one who had wiped his sweat—charged at Long Kor, and the two became embroiled in a melee of fists and legs. The other, a lanky fellow a head taller than Yang, lowered his stare towards Yang. Smirking, he gestured a 'come on' with his hand, palm facing up.

'Small boy, you want to fight me?' he sneered.

Yang did not reply. He felt the rush of blood pumping in his chest, its heat emanating from his face. His breathing quickened.

'Come on,' the fellow continued to taunt. 'Why? Scared ah? Your Ba never taught you how to fight?'

With an animal cry, Yang charged at the enemy. He jumped and lashed out mercilessly with a hard kick. The enemy flew back and landed on the ground with a thump. Shocked and bewildered, he tried to get back onto his feet. Just as he rose on one knee, a series of fiery punches to his face in quick succession grounded him again. The taste of warm blood met his lips.

'Yes, my Ba never taught me how to fight,' a panting, raspy voice hissed.

Pinned to the ground by a leg, he saw the raising of an arm and a clenched fist coming down on him. He squeezed his eyes shut and waited for the blow.

When the blow did not come, he opened his eyes. The boy's arm was being held in the air by his older comrade, who was shaking his head as he looked intently at the boy. After a few seconds, the boy released his leg.

The defeated young man stumbled to his feet and hobbled out of the alley with his mate. At the end of the alley, he turned back to glance, just momentarily, at the young man whose anger seemed so relentless. Fiery almost. Then they were gone.

Long Kor stood beside Yang, both panting in the aftermath of the brawl. The sky was darkening; the light was hobbling away along with their supposed enemies. The setting sun cast two shadows, one slightly shorter than the other, along the sombre back alley. A smear of blood stained the grey cement of the lane.

Long Kor turned to glance at his younger friend, a hint of unease in his eyes.

'We fight to protect. To defend,' he said slowly. 'To defeat, yes. But not to . . .' his words trailed off. There was a pause before he continued, 'You can go to jail. Be careful.'

Yang felt a need to meet the gaze of his friend, his *dai kor*, the elder brother who had taken him under his wing. Yet he could not. He had crushed his rival, but in the dim alley in which they stood, it seemed as though there lurked an unseen enemy more sinister than the opponent he had just defeated.

He looked down at the dirt and the rubbish strewn on the ground. He heard Long Kor's steps and his voice beckoning. Numbly, he edged forward.

Part Two

Water

Light and life gifted by the sun
Yet scars are overflowing
Washing the parched land
Into brave, lonely seas

***

1975

Chapter 10

Snow's fingers gripped the pencil as its tip brushed against the paper, on which the semblance of a handkerchief tree began to appear. Looking up briefly at the tree in the distance, on the other side of the riverbank, she became aware of the dampness on her school uniform where her weight bore down on the grass patch on which she sat. Her knees drawn up, she squinted in renewed concentration at the drawing paper resting on her legs, the strokes of her pencil lighter now, as she sketched the light-coloured, new leaves hanging in limp tassels from the branches. Soft handkerchiefs hanging all over the tree.

A sudden splash from the river. A soft squeal of delight as she scoured her school bag, pulling out an old tape recorder. A black nostril, white whiskers, and a brown head poked out of the murky water, squeaking as it called to its companions. More furry brown heads made their appearance. One held a fish in its mouth. Her eyes glinted as a smile softened her face. There had been afternoons in the past when she had been rewarded with sightings of otters, but this afternoon, she had come prepared with a tape recorder. This evening, she would be able to let her mother listen to the recorded squeaking of the otters.

No one else was at this secluded part of the Kallang River, tucked away as it was from the Kallang Gasworks and the riverside kampongs with their wooden huts raised on stilts. The water was dirty—empty bottles, tin cans, discarded banana peel and all kinds of rubbish floated along. The cool drift of the water as it brushed against the muddy banks drew her into its lull, beckoning her to blend into its flowing melody as the afternoon sun beat down on the soft, leafy fabric of the handkerchiefs fluttering in the light breeze as they hung on the tree across the river.

She looked up at the ripening mangoes hanging from the mango tree beside her and breathed in their fragrance. Putting her drawing aside, she cast cautious glances all around. Then, with a leap, she caught hold of the lowest branch of the tree and heaved herself into its foliage.

Yang watched the beads of perspiration roll down Ah Pui's neck as his friend walked just ahead of him on the narrow, muddy path. 'I found a nice place to swim. Just what we need,' Ah Pui panted, half turning towards his friend walking behind. Yang remained silent as he stepped along sullenly.

'Ooi, say something, can or not? Why are you always so glum?' Ah Pui continued.

'Mmm.'

'*Cheh*! Dunno what's with you nowadays!' Ah Pui heaved in exasperation.

They could hear the distant sound of water as they neared the river. Ah Pui pulled his sweat-soaked shirt off, using this to wipe his face. Then, he stopped abruptly in his tracks, causing Yang to bump into him from the back.

'Pui! What the—'

'Sshhh!'

Ah Pui raised his palm to shoulder-level and, with his fingers motioning forward, gestured to his friend to come take a look. The two of them stood gazing at a mango tree near the river in the distance.

The mango tree shook, then stopped. The tree stood still for a moment, after which the shuddering began again, similarly halting a few seconds later. The solo voice of a girl rang out, cutting through the hot, humid afternoon air, giving life to a song they had heard time and again when they were living in the kampong long ago:

> *Burung kakatua (The cockatoo)*
> *Hinggap di jendela (Sits on the window sill)*
> *Nenek sudah tua (My grandmother is already old)*
> *Giginya tinggal dua. (And she only has two teeth!)*

> *Tredung, tredung, tredung tra la la*
> *Tredung, tredung, tredung tra la la*
> *Tredung, tredung, tredung tra la la*
> *Tredung, tredung, tredung tra la la*
> *Burung kakatua!*

Ah Pui gave his friend a nudge as they listened to the song. Memories of their childhood washed into their hearts, powerful waves which held in their ebb and flow the nights in the kampong when neighbours would sing folk songs or tell stories as they gathered outside their attap huts.

The voice drew them on towards the tree. They peered into its thick foliage. Someone was crouching on a branch, reaching out for the hanging fruit—a teenage girl in her school uniform was singing the familiar Indonesian folk song as she plucked the fruit with her back towards them. She tossed the plucked mangoes onto the ground, where there was a small heap of the fruit already.

She turned around. The singing stopped as she gasped. Two young men, one fat and one lean, were standing below the tree, peering up at her. The fat one was bare-bodied, his T-shirt clutched in his hand. Hastily, she jumped onto the ground, her face breaking into a frown at their dubious, staring intrusion.

'Why are you staring at me?' she questioned.

The two gave each other a brief glance before turning back to face her, still not uttering a word. They did not know what to say—what should they say?

An inexplicable anger began coursing through her; they had been staring at her in the same manner in which pesky people had stared at her Ma all these years. Grabbing the mangoes and stones on the ground, she hurled those at the two intruders.

Bewilderment on their faces, the two young men shielded themselves with their arms as the stones and mangoes pelted forth. A stone hit Ah Pui smack on his bare stomach. He howled in pain, bending over, grimacing. He turned to Yang, huffing 'Run!' before bolting.

A ripe, juicy mango slammed into Yang, smashing its flesh and fragrance onto his shirt. He did not run; instead, he stood firm amid the tumultuous raining of mangoes and stones. In battle, one only ran if one was afraid of the opponent; it was equivalent to admitting defeat or acknowledging wrongdoing.

When she ran out of mangoes, the girl stood staring daggers at him, panting. In her eyes he saw intense pluck—it was the first time he locked eyes with a girl in this way.

Suddenly, she jumped up with a yelp. With shouts of 'Ouch!', she started slapping her own hands and legs. Yang realized what was plaguing her. Ants. Ants were crawling all over her and biting her.

Dropping his haversack on the ground, he grabbed her hand and ran towards the river, pulling her along. In they plunged, and as they submerged, the drowning ants floated. He did not let go of her hand, not knowing if she could swim. His feet touched the riverbed; the river was, fortunately, not deep.

Minutes later, they climbed out of the water, with him still holding onto her hand. They collapsed onto the grass, soaked and panting. He glanced at her, dripping with muddy water. A twig had become entangled in her cropped, wet hair.

Remembering that he had a spare T-shirt in his haversack—spare attire enabled him to change out of his muddied or bloodied clothes before he went home after a gang fight—he got up, took the spare T-shirt out from his bag, and held it out to her. She looked disconcertedly at her soaked school uniform, then somewhat apprehensively at him and the T-shirt he offered. Finally, hesitantly, she accepted it.

He turned with a quick nod at her and strode away, drenched in river water laced with mango juice and, despite the wash, still exuding hints of mango fragrance.

Chapter 11

She walked briskly, acutely conscious that it was a man's T-shirt she was wearing. The oversized shirt hung loosely on her slim frame, its sleeves almost reaching her elbows. She made a mental map of the safest route to take, in order to reach her home with minimal notice.

The scene at the river played out repeatedly in her thoughts. Perhaps the two young men had not meant any harm, even though they were staring at her. If they did, surely the one who did not run away could have assaulted her, instead of helping her with the ant attack, and subsequently offering a shirt to her. Not to mention that he got himself soaking wet because of her. She would not have been able to fight him off, and help was far away in that secluded part of the river. She had not seen aggression in their faces, nor in their actions.

Reaching the block of flats in Kallang where she lived, she avoided her family's provision shop on the ground floor, taking instead the longer route by the back of the building. Up the lift, then quietly unlocking the front door, she took a peek inside.

No one was home. She grabbed some clean clothes and was soon safe in the bathroom.

As she pulled the T-shirt over her head, she paused at the faint scent of masculine perspiration embedded in the fabric. It was the first time she had worn a man's shirt. She found the sour-sweet, musky odour strangely alluring, making her heart race in a flustered frenzy, and she hurriedly put it aside.

After a shower, she made her way down to the provision shop.

'Nenek!' she called out to her grandmother.

Seeing her 15-year-old granddaughter, the plump old lady, seated at the counter, beamed.

'Hello sayang. *Sekolah sudah habis*, school is over?'

Snow nodded. '*Bapak, Ibu dimana?*' she asked where her father and mother were.

Nenek pointed with her chin towards the last isle of the shop. Snow walked over. Her father was squatting in front of the large refrigerator, replenishing the cartons of milk inside. He looked up when he heard his daughter call out, 'Ba!'

'Xue'er, you're back,' he acknowledged her call and, with some difficulty, straightened himself. She helped him place the remaining cartons of milk in the fridge. 'Ma is at the back,' he continued.

Craning her neck, she saw her mother at the end of the isle, placing cans of luncheon meat on a shelf in the slow, careful manner typical of her actions. Ba now ambled out of the shop, pulling out his packet of cigarettes as he walked. He was going for a smoke, as he frequently did all these years.

Snow approached her Ma and, without a word, began helping to stack the cans of meat on the shelf. Ma smiled.

It pained Snow to see how slow and arduous it was for Ma, having to feel with her hands for the shelf, its sharp edges, and other items on it. Ma always insisted on doing some work in the shop, on making herself useful, on troubling others as little as possible. As a child, Snow would watch as Ma learnt to read and write in Braille; mother and daughter spent hours huddled over pages which, at that time, seemed to Snow like thousands of stars upon a white sky, bringing hope to her mother's dark world.

'Ma, next time wait for me or Ba to stack the food.'

'I can do it,' Ma replied.

Remembering the tape recorder she had brought along, Snow said excitedly, 'Ma, listen to this. You'll like it!' She pressed the play button. At first, only background noise could be heard, but soon the squeaks of the otters were discernible.

'Oh?'

'Otters. At the river.'

Ma stretched out her hand; Snow edged forward so her mother could touch her face. She gazed at her mother, at the disfigured face she had grown up with; at the distorted, scarred skin where it should have been smooth and supple; at the unseeing eyes.

Her mother had been badly burned in that destructive fire many years ago, when Snow had been just a year old and their family lived in Kampong Bukit Ho Swee. The burns had left her mother disfigured. And blind.

She would have liked the warmth of her mother's touch to linger a little longer, but a plump, middle-aged woman they had not seen before strolled into the aisle; a first-time customer who looked from the food on the shelves to the scars on Ma's face. A loud gasp; then a wide-eyed, mouth-gaping stare. 'Aiyo! You gave me such a fright! Why's your face so scary?' she blurted out.

Snow heard the slight quickening in her mother's breathing, saw the lowering of her mother's face as her fingers gripped the fabric of her skirt. Rude, angry words would have tumbled out, were it not for Nenek calling her from the front of the shop, 'Xue'er, come help Hua Ah-Yee carry her things.'

'Coming!' Snow shouted, giving the woman a sharp glare before walking hand in hand with Ma to the counter. Hua Ah-Yee was a kind, elderly lady living in the block, who frequented their shop. Snow picked up the two bags of groceries, greeting Hua Ah-Yee cheerfully, 'Hua Ah-Yee, let me help you.'

The old lady, buoyed by the effusive warmth and sincerity of the young lady hugging the two bags of groceries, chatted jovially with her. As they walked towards her flat, the old lady turned towards her young companion.

'You and your family are such warm, good-hearted people. May I ask, what happened to your mother, how did she get burned?' she sighed, pausing. 'My heart aches when I see her. You are so kind and pretty. Your mother must have been too. So sad to see her like that.'

Snow slowed down; her gaze lowered as they came to a halt. 'She was trying to escape, like everyone else. From the fire,' she said quietly. 'I was very young then. My Nenek escaped, carrying me. My Ma was with a neighbour, trying to carry whatever they could with them. It was very chaotic, so they don't remember clearly. My Ma says she was hit by something from behind, and she fell. Her hair caught fire ...'

Her voice trailed off. The old lady placed her hand on her arm, giving a gentle squeeze. Snow accepted the affection with a pained smile.

Later, when she stood alone, leaning against the parapet, an ache gnawed inside her. The old lady's well-meaning words, that her mother must have been pretty, stirred up a cauldron of pent-up emotions which had been imposing themselves upon her with increasing intensity in recent years. Resentment barged into her teenage consciousness like an unruly companion who had waited for his time, had stood on the sidelines in her younger years, before finally deeming it opportune to brand his tumultuous passions into her being.

She had never known what her mother really looked like. And her mother could not—would never be able to—see the face of the young woman she was growing into.

Chapter 12

Yang dragged Ah Pui by his arm into the alley behind the coffee shop, ignoring Ah Pui's protestations, and loosening his grip only when they had reached the back alley. He gave Ah Pui the indignant glare of a friend who'd been deserted by the flight of his supposed buddy in the face of an attack.

Ah Pui winced; he scratched his head. 'Sorry lah, brother. I also got hit by the stones okay! You yourself didn't run away, not my fault what!'

'Maybe she was scared cos you took off your shirt!'

'But we didn't do anything, what! I just wanted to go swimming. Then suddenly there's this girl there. I didn't mean to—'

'I know, I know.'

'So, what happened after that?'

'She had ants all over, biting her. I pulled her to the river, and we jumped in.'

'Oooh,' Ah Pui whistled, raising his arm in dramatic storytelling fashion. 'Boy saves girl from attack,' he lowered his voice to a whisper, 'Uh hmm, never mind that the enemies were tiny little ants—'

'Stop it. It's all your fault.'

Ah Pui draped his arm around his friend's shoulder, a wicked smile on his face. 'She's *chio*, pretty, no?'

Yang gave a whack to the back of his friend's head, and Ah Pui scampered back to the coffee shop with Yang giving chase.

The coffee shop owned by Ah Pui's family was starting to fill up with the evening crowd. Yang and Ah Pui had just completed their mandatory National Service. Ah Pui was embarking on higher education shortly; Yang, having passed his GCE 'O' level exams, had not yet figured out what to do next. Meanwhile, he worked at Ah Pui's coffee shop, helping out with anything and everything, from taking orders to cooking, from washing the dishes to consolidating the accounts with Ah Pui.

Yang went about his chores wordlessly, fulfilling the tasks required of him without engaging in much of the casual talk among the other stallholders and workers.

At about 8 P.M., a group of three burly men sauntered in, making their presence conspicuous with loud grunts and laughter. One of them looked around and, spotting Yang, walked over.

'You,' the man pointed at Yang, barking loudly, 'my men tell me you were selling your pirated cassettes in our territory.'

An apprehensive hush fell upon the place, as the crowd in the coffee shop turned to look.

Yang returned the glare of the man. 'Don't you create a scene here,' he growled, pointing towards the back lane, 'We settle this outside.'

Yang sized them up as they faced him menacingly in the dark alley, the same one in which he and Ah Pui had stood in the daylight. Of the three, two were taller and bigger than he was.

He took a risk the previous weekend when he had decided to sell his cassettes in 'their territory', where business was brisk. He could earn twice the amount he would normally earn in other areas. Now, it was time to pay for his gamble.

The one who had spoken in the coffee shop started to crack his knuckles. 'You dare to sell your things in our area, huh?' he snarled. 'I've heard of you. You're with Chen Long. I heard you're very daring. But you know what? Daring people get into trouble.'

He threw a punch at Yang, who dodged, landing a kick on his opponent instead. The two other men charged at him. He felt a kick to his chest, and a sharp pain on his right arm. Another kick sent him crashing to the ground. There was a glint from a penknife brandished by his assailant; then blood trickling down his arm, where a slit had been made in his flesh.

As he lay on the tarmac, a fiery stone began churning inside him, gathering speed, amassing energy with each quickened breath he took, creating powerful surges of heat in the blood coursing through his veins, till finally, with a cry of war, he jumped back onto his feet, leapt in the air, lashed out with his legs in lightning speed.

The man who had slashed his arm fell to the ground. Stunned, the other two looked momentarily at each other before launching a counterattack. They punched. He kicked. They dodged. He punched. They fell to the ground. They got up. He fell to the ground. He got up.

Ten minutes later, the hunters and the hunted persisted in their confrontation, panting, neither conceding defeat, nor claiming victory. Eventually, the leader, without taking his eyes off Yang, signalled to his gang with a wave of his chin. They turned to go, the leader snarling at Yang, 'You watch out,' before leaving.

Quiet returned once more to the murky alley in which a bruised young man continued to stand. Coming out of the shadows, Ah Pui walked over.

'You okay?' he asked, a concerned look on his face, his hand on Yang's shoulder, 'Your hand is bleeding.'

Yang nodded. Pushing Ah Pui's hand away, he hobbled out of the alley without a word.

When Yang stepped into his flat, his Ma was on the telephone. She often spoke for hours on end over the phone—it had been this way all these years—gossiping about this person and that; the deeper she pricked someone else, the more bearable the thorn felt in her own flesh.

They had moved to a slightly larger, two-room flat in the adjacent block a few years ago, thanks to the income he and Dai Kah Jie pooled together. Yee Kah Jie had married and now lived with her husband's family. Dai Kah Jie, who sold vegetables at a nearby wet market, shared the bedroom with Ma, while he slept in the living room.

'Jie,' he greeted Dai Kah Jie.

She looked up from where she was folding the clothes in the bedroom, her gaze lingering on his bruised face, on his bleeding arm where a cut had been inflicted. Putting the clothes aside, she opened a drawer, took out a bottle of ointment, held it out to him; a simple gesture which belied the sadness in her eyes. Accepting the ointment, he said, 'I'm fine. Don't worry.'

There came the sound of the phone receiver being placed back on its cradle. Ma walked over, the scar on her face still visible but less conspicuous after so many years. She took a brief glance at him before walking into the bedroom, saying curtly as she did, '*Yao da gao. Sui zai!* Fighting again, rascal!'

He put his bag down; went to the bathroom without a word. Dai Kah Jie's heart ached as her gaze followed her brother—a hardened silence was often all that greeted them, as if he went about his life sealed in a space no one could enter.

That night, as he lay on his mattress in the living room, his thoughts went back to the girl he had met by the river, to their unpleasant encounter which must have left her with a terrible first impression of him and Ah Pui. He wished it had not been so; in her eyes he had seen a tenacity which he respected, which he felt drawn to, and which—for some reason—evoked a tingling sensation in him that was as strange as it was warm.

Chapter 13

The following week, Yang found himself walking towards the Kallang River one afternoon, when the lunch crowds had dissipated from the coffee shop, and he had some free time before the evening bustle.

He did not know why he headed towards the part of the river where he had met the girl. Perhaps he needed to sort out his thoughts in a quiet place. Ma had been nagging at him to get a proper job. 'Don't disgrace me after all the money spent on your studies,' she had snapped. Dai Kah Jie had worked hard to support the family all these years, especially after Ba stopped sending money abruptly, when he was fifteen.

They did not know why Ba had stopped sending money; nor did they know where he was or how to contact him. They did not even know if he was alive or dead. Before he was enlisted in the army, when he was still at school, Yang had supplemented the family's income by working at Ah Pui's coffee shop in the afternoons and evenings after school, and by selling pirated cassettes on weekends. He had learnt the tricks of the trade from Long Kor, after which he started selling these cassettes on his own.

Reaching the banks of the river, he sat down. He seemed to hear again the sound of her voice as she sang. He again saw her eyes as she glared at him, her wet hair, the twig caught in it. Why was he thinking of her? he asked himself, as he tried to shake the image of her face away.

He listened to the soft, calming sound of the flowing water as it rippled over the stones on the riverbed. The murkiness of the water struck him. Garbage and carcasses of dead fish were strewn everywhere, giving rise to a stench similar to the one he had grown up with in his kampong, before it was burnt down.

After a while, he got up and made his way back to the coffee shop. It was nearing dinner time and there was work to be done.

Two weeks later, he found himself back at the river. Again, he had wandered there without knowing why. Again, he sat there alone, in the company of the nonchalant humming of the water and the tufts of tall, thirsty grass—for there had been no rain in the past two weeks, leaving patches of brown where it had been green two weeks ago. Drooping blades conveyed their reminiscence of better days when they had stood tall and proud. The sun, as if chided by the tranquil river, flitted meekly where it met the gentle, undulating water.

A sudden splash. A brown head with whiskers emerged from the surface of the water. Soon more heads popped out. Squeaks now accompanied the water's song, as a family of otters swam and splashed, calling out to one another as they did so. Soon they began swimming away, leaving behind a young one happily eating a fish. Realizing it was now alone, it squeaked in distress as it swam in search of its family.

A drop of water landed on his arm. Then another. And another. He looked up at the dark clouds which had gathered rapidly in the sky.

The raindrops now pelted down with increasing haste, as if they knew they had made the parched earth wait under the fiery sun for too long, as if anxious to make amends for their tarry. And the outpouring of tears from the heavens washed the tired earth, renewing her sounds, her scents, making her skin soft and supple once more.

Yang stood up and started running. He was soaked by the time he got to a nearby block of flats. Not having been to this part of Kallang before, he looked around as he took shelter there. He walked towards a provision shop at the end of the block. Rainwater dripped from his hair, his clothes; squelched from the holes in his worn shoes as he approached the shop entrance.

An old lady looked up from where she sat behind the cash counter. Seeing the young man drenched by the downpour, she smiled affably, exclaiming, '*Alamak*, you're all wet, son. Come in, come in.'

Yang nodded in gratitude. The old lady's face and voice seemed very familiar. As he stepped into the shop, the rainwater continued to drip, gathering in small puddles on the cement floor near his feet. Feeling as apologetic as he was embarrassed, he searched in his mind for what he should say as he looked around the shop and back at the old lady.

Suddenly, he remembered. 'Nenek, is that you?' he asked, a smile lighting up his face. 'I'm Yang, from the kampong.'

The old lady blinked for a moment as she tried to recall who this young man was.

'Yang,' she repeated, searching her memory. She scrutinized his face. Then her face lit up. 'Ahh! Yah! Now I remember! Your father used to deliver Pepsi to our shop, right?'

Yang nodded, trying to conceal the sudden, sharp burn in his chest with the raking up of these memories.

'How is your father?' Nenek asked.

The well-intentioned question felt like a sting in his stomach, where it smouldered like burning embers. He looked down momentarily. How was his father? He did not know; did not want to know, he told himself. Forcing a smile, he replied, 'He's fine, thanks for your concern.'

A middle-aged lady walked over haltingly, her hands guiding her feet as they felt for objects to her front and sides. Yang was taken aback by her face—it was badly disfigured, her eyes unseeing. Her face did not look like a human face at all.

'That's Aunty Su Mei, my daughter-in-law, remember?' Nenek said, her voice becoming softer, her eyes becoming slightly distant as she continued, 'Aunty Su Mei was burned in the fire.'

Yang greeted the lady, whose warmth and kindness to him as a child he remembered well. '*Ni hao*, hope you're well, Mei Ah-Yee.' He did not know what else to say as he stood awkwardly at the entrance to the shop.

Just then, a girl's chirpy voice rang out from behind him.

'Nenek! Ma, I'm back!'

He turned around. It was her—the girl he had met at the river.

She drew back when she saw him.

'It's okay,' Nenek said to her. 'This young man was our neighbour back in the kampong. His name is Lee Yang.' Then she told Yang, 'This is my granddaughter, Xue'er.'

The girl's tension seemed to ease a little as she shifted her gaze from his face to her Nenek's smile and back to his face again. A few awkward seconds passed before Nenek spoke again.

'We haven't seen him since the fire.He was a small boy then. He was caught in the rain, came here for shelter, so we meet again. But ooh la la, here we're talking and he's all wet! Xue'er, better get him some dry clothes.' She turned to Yang, 'You better get dry first. Come here to look for us again, okay?'

Snow cast a sidelong glance at him as she nodded an acknowledgment to her grandmother. She did not utter a word about the encounter at the river. 'Come with me,' she said as she walked out of the shop.

They walked without exchanging a word to the lobby. He badly wanted to explain why he and Ah Pui were staring at her that day, but did not know where to begin, unprepared as he was for this second meeting with her. They stood waiting wordlessly, both facing the lift door, she keeping her distance.

They went into the lift; she pressed the button. He did not know why, but his heart was beating as if on a drumroll; as the little box they stood in moved upward, so did an inexplicable heat—not the kind he felt when he fought with other men, but a different kind, one of intense embarrassment—push upwards inside him, till he felt almost certain she could hear the mortifying 'thump-thump-thump'. Droplets of water plopped from his soaked clothes onto the floor amid the frisson of combustible tremulousness wringing his nerves—here he was, nothing but water, and here he was, nothing but tinder.

Finally, as they stepped out of the lift, he blurted out, 'Sorry. For that day, I mean. At the river. My friend just wanted to go for a swim,' he paused, 'We, we didn't know. My friend took off his shirt cos it was hot. We didn't mean to stare, didn't mean any harm …'

She eyed him suspiciously for a moment. 'Okay. I got upset cos the two of you were staring at me, and your friend wasn't wearing his shirt … you know,' she replied. 'Sorry. About throwing the stones and mangoes, I mean.'

'It's okay, I understand.'

'Wait here,' she instructed as she opened the front door to her flat. After a few minutes she emerged holding a T-shirt—his T-shirt.

'Here,' she handed him the shirt. 'It's yours anyway. I was wondering how to return it to you.' She blushed a little. 'Thank you. For helping me, with the ants. And for the T-shirt.'

They stood facing each other, glances diverted. It struck him that in both their encounters, he had stood before her soaked, dripping with water.

Finally, he said, 'The river's a bit dirty, but still nice. I was there today. That's why I got caught in the rain. And I saw some otters.'

She looked at him and smiled and, for a fleeting moment, their eyes met.

Chapter 14

Ah Pui wiped his perspiration on the sleeve of his shirt as he trekked towards the playground. This must be the one, he thought as he halted to catch his breath, wondering why Yang had asked to meet him at this playground in Kallang under the heat of the afternoon sun. The coffee shop was closed today, and he would much rather have remained at home.

Two teenage girls were sitting on the dragon's tail at the playground, looking in the opposite direction. Yang was nowhere in sight. Ah Pui slowed down his pace, treading lightly now. One of the girls began turning in his direction. He gasped, almost tripping. In a frenzy, he shot towards safety behind the head of the dragon, where he hid. It was her—the girl in the mango tree. He would be dead meat if she saw him. Petrified, he inched farther behind the head of the fearless dragon, keeping as still as he could, closing his eyes, the beads of perspiration trickling down his face.

Without warning, someone smacked his head from behind. He lost his balance, toppled onto the sand, and with a yelp rolled over till he lay flat on his tummy. He spun around—his supposed good friend Yang was standing there, leaning against the dragon's head with his arms folded, a look of admonishment on his face. The two girls straightened in surprise. A smile gradually spread across the mango girl's face as she looked at the young man sprawled on the sand in front of her. The other girl chuckled.

'Hello,' the mango girl teased, 'Nice to meet you, again.'

He quickly jumped back onto his feet, brushing the sand off in as dignified a manner as he could, feeling highly mortified.

'Um,' he fumbled as he scratched his head, 'Sorry. For staring at you that day. No offence, okay? I didn't mean anything.'

'I know. Your friend explained,' she replied, her face lit by a smile.

Ah Pui saw that her eyes shone with effusive friendliness. He turned to glare at Yang, who now walked over, jabbing a finger at his friend's shoulder as he said, 'That was your punishment.'

'For what?'

'For getting all of us into trouble that day, then running away.'

Ah Pui gave Yang an amicable punch in the chest. 'Okay, okay. My fault.' He turned towards the girls. 'Later we go eat at the street stalls, okay? My treat ah, Miss—?'

'My friends call me Snow, and this is my friend, Meiyun.'

The four of them made their way to the stalls nearby. Yang, unlike his friends, did not talk much. At the stalls, Snow began striking up conversations with the hawkers and, in a matter of minutes, was chatting with them as if she'd known them for years.

Yang observed a sparkle in her warm exuberance that was, in fact, quite the opposite of her name. Her friend Meiyun was chatty, but Snow was more spirited than chatty, with a sincerity in the way she looked at and spoke to others, something of a genuine warmth and authenticity in the way she reached out. Perhaps, it was an authenticity he had never seen in his own mother.

Coming to a stall selling fruits, Ah Pui picked up a mango and, with an impish grin, breathed in the fruity fragrance in an exaggerated fashion before shoving it into Yang's hand, exclaiming, 'Veree nice mango, ya?'

The thrilled stallholder chimed in, 'Ya! Mango nice! Papaya also nice! Want?' He offered a papaya to Ah Pui, who looked from the smooth skin of the papaya to the long scar on his friend's arm, the one inflicted by a penknife during the recent fight in the alley. The hopeful stallholder continued to hold up the unblemished papaya. Ah Pui shook his head. The stallholder chose another smooth-skinned papaya; again, the plump customer shook his head.

Finally, Ah Pui picked up a papaya with a long scar on its skin. He held it up beside Yang, scrutinizing the man and the fruit, nodding with satisfaction. 'This one!' he said to the puzzled stallholder, who scratched his head and raised his brows. 'This one?'

Ah Pui slapped Yang's shoulders, then slapped the papaya. 'Ya, this one!' he affirmed. 'Mango and papaya go well together, no?' he chuckled, grabbing the mango from Yang and bringing it close to the papaya. 'Papaya, mango! Mango, papaya!'

Yang scowled at his buddy who seemed bent on being annoying. Meiyun walked over.

'You stupid or what? This one?' she asked Ah Pui incredulously, pointing to the scar on the papaya.

'Aiya, you don't know lah!' Ah Pui retorted. 'Outside not nice doesn't mean inside not nice!'

Meiyun picked up the first papaya the stallholder had offered them. 'This one!' she told the stallholder. Ah Pui pushed her hand aside, holding up the scarred papaya. 'No, this one!' he insisted.

They went on in this manner, each refusing to budge, as the stallholder looked from one to the other in bewilderment. Finally, Yang took both papayas from them, placed the papayas back on the rack and, frowning, dragged them away from the stall.

Snow called out to them from a stall selling *you tiao*, the long dough sticks fried in oil. The stall owner was telling her that he'd been unable to sell much of his dough fritters, and that his sickly wife was at home. Yang and Ah Pui listened, skeptical, as the hawker sighed and shook his head.

After a brief silence, Snow gave the elderly man a resolute smile. 'We will buy all your dough fritters,' she said cheerfully, then glanced at Ah Pui, 'Right Ah Pui?'

Ah Pui's jaws dropped. His widened eyes looked from Snow to the hawker to the dozens of dough fritters on his cart. 'A … All?' he stammered.

'Why not?' Snow asked buoyantly. 'You can afford it, right?'

'Of course, I can afford it!' Ah Pui crossed his arms, putting on an air of indignance.

'Kum sia, kum sia! Thank you, thank you! You are so kind!' the beaming hawker wasted no time in seizing the good fortune that had come upon him. With one hand picking up his metal tongs and the other holding open a paper bag, he deftly shoved the sticks into the bag. One stick, two sticks, three, four. Next bag. One stick, two sticks, three, four.

Ah Pui looked on, wide-eyed, blinking; Yang looked on, arms crossed, lips upturned in amusement. Soon they were carrying bags of dough fritters in their haversacks, imagining the sickly feeling from eating too many dough sticks fried by a man with a sickly wife at home.

Chapter 15

In the weeks that followed, the four friends often went to the hawkers' stalls. At times, they accompanied Snow back to her provision shop.

One day, as Yang and Ah Pui walked with Snow towards her shop, a young couple walked out, the man carrying a bag of items just purchased, the young woman carrying a look of disgust on her face.

'Did you see that woman in the shop? Did you see her face?' the woman asked the man. Snow stopped in her tracks as the couple walked past them.

'I've never seen such an ugly woman before!' the woman continued. 'She looks so repulsive, I almost puked!'

'Ya, not like my girl, so pretty,' the man said as he slid his hand onto her hips.

Yang turned to look at Snow. Her fists were clenched, her brows furrowed. Her breaths became short and quick. Suddenly, she turned around, strode towards the couple, grabbed the bag the man was carrying and flung it onto the ground.

'If she's so repulsive, don't buy her things!' she rebuked them loudly, looking the woman in the eye.

Confounded, the couple regarded their items strewn on the ground. Anger was soon strewn across their faces.

'You! What's your problem, huh? Why throw our things for no reason?' the woman hollered, staring at Snow. 'I was just saying the truth. That woman looks hideous. You better pick up our things!' She turned towards the man, tugging his arm. He glowered at Snow, taking a step forward.

Yang blocked the man with his arm. Enraged, the man turned to face Yang. The two grabbed each other by the shirt. Each glared at the other, daring the other to a test of strength, as they held tightly onto the opponent's clothing, refusing to let go.

Ah Pui swiftly pushed himself between them, trying to separate the two, using his body weight to pry them apart. He then hurriedly picked the items up, shoved them into the bag, and thrust it into the man's chest.

'No need to fight, okay? You have your items back now!' Ah Pui called out to the couple as he pulled Yang and Snow away. The couple walked off in a huff.

Snow, Yang, and Ah Pui stood on the pavement, panting slightly from the scuffle. Abruptly, Snow swivelled away from them and ran in the direction of the river.

Snow sat on a grass patch near the water, looking at the trees on the other side of the river. She pulled her knees towards her chest, wrapping her arms around them. The sting of the young couple's words lodged inside her and would not dissipate. As she sat alone with the river, the dam broke and released its watery anger into the crevices of her eyes.

A light breeze trod across the water, carrying with it the murmurs of the leaves and the whiff of muddy grass.

A mild stench of decomposing rubbish wafted along, as it always did.

She did not notice the approaching footfall. A shadow appeared beside her. She hastily wiped her tears with the back of her hand, then turned around, looked up. Yang stood a short distance behind her. He walked over, sat down beside her. From his bag, he took out two cans of chrysanthemum tea and held one out to her. Parched, she accepted his gesture of kindness, of friendship.

They sat there in the embrace of the late afternoon sun, neither uttering a word. He gazed at the handkerchief tree in the distance—perhaps he should offer her a handkerchief, but he did not have one. Never carried one. He now understood why stares from others stoked her so badly. Her mother had been burned in the fire—like his mother, though her mother was burned much more severely. Both their mothers bore the scars on their faces. Her father stayed. His father did not. Perhaps these scars would continue to reverberate in their lives; his and hers.

A deep emptiness filled him when he thought of his father; of how he had sat wordlessly beside his father outside their attap house; of how his father had provided for the family; of how he had left them without a word.

The soft notes of a melody sounded. He turned to look at her—she was holding a harmonica from which the music flowed. It was the same song. *Burung kakak tua.*

As Yang sat there beside Snow and her music, beside the river and her earthly melody, it seemed to him he was being blessed with one of the most beautiful moments in his solitary life.

A brown squirrel scurried down the trunk of a rain tree, perching on a large, protruding root, scanning the horizon for danger before scampering across the grass onto another tree. A collared kingfisher darted from a tree to the water and back to the tree again—a brilliant blue bursting forth in an instant that would linger not in time but in memory.

Snow's eyes lit up. She turned towards Yang.

'Did you see that?'

He nodded, noticing the spirited glint returning to her eyes. Unlike the iciness her name alluded to, the warmth and sincerity in her gaze drew him in yet again to those eyes which seemed to offer nothing but genuine good intentions.

'Will you walk with me?' she asked him.

They began strolling along the river. Soon, rows of attap houses on the riverbank came into sight. Her footsteps came to a halt.

'You remember your kampong? Our kampong? Was it something like those attap houses?'

'I remember. Ya, something like that.'

'You remember the fire?'

He nodded.

'My Ma. She was burnt in the fire. That's why … her face …' her voice trailed off.

He thought of his own Ma but did not say anything. Perhaps there wasn't a need to let her know. After all, his life had been estranged from his Ba, and, in a way, from his Ma as well. He might still be living under the same roof as his Ma, yet their lives were as apart as their living quarters were close.

'Why didn't your Ma escape?' he asked.

It was a while before she spoke. 'She was trying to,' she said softly, her gaze resting on the attap houses in the distance. 'Something hit her from behind, and she fell.'

They continued along the riverbank. Seeing her downcast eyes, he picked up a stone and held it out to her.

'Remember?' he asked. A smile crept onto his face. She looked from the stone in his outstretched hand to the slightly cheeky smile stretched out beneath his deep, intense eyes. It was the first time she had seen him smile in this manner. Playful. Unrestrained.

In the time that she had known him, he had always been somewhat reticent. While thoughtful and unflinching where his friend had been careless and faint-hearted, there was always something holding him back, as if he had made up his mind a long time ago to remain on the sidelines, watching the world but not wanting to engage. Now, for once, the heavy fog had lifted, if only for a fleeting moment.

Taking the stone from him, she returned his teasing smile; raised her arm in a mischievous pretence of aiming at him. She then turned, threw the pebble into the water.

'So, how did *you* escape from the fire?'

'Me?' he asked, with a slightly embarrassed smile as he recalled his boyish silliness. 'I grabbed my two chickens and ran.'

'Your two chickens?'

'Don't ask me why. Everyone else grabbed their valuables. But I grabbed my chickens.' He picked up another stone, which he tossed into the river. In a more serious tone, he continued, 'When I went back with my Ba the day after the fire, everything had been burnt. Even our pig, Ah Poop, was burnt.'

A somewhat wistful look had come into his eyes.

'Ah Poop?' she asked, amused by the name.

'Yup,' he gave a light chuckle. 'I called him 'Ah Poop' cos he used to eat our poop every day.'

She grinned at the thought of Ah Poop the pig. Seeing her smile, he felt a strange lightness of being, as if the layers of armour he had built around himself over the years were momentarily lifted, and he was once again the boy in the wooden shed talking to his friend the pig, with nothing but awe for the mighty wonders of this world.

Chapter 16

The months plodded along into a new year. Snow would occasionally go to Ah Pui's coffee shop to look for Yang and Ah Pui in the afternoons, after school. If she stayed for dinner, Yang would walk her home thereafter. The two of them would meet often at the river.

On one such occasion, he saw her swimming in the river when he arrived. Intrigued, he hid behind some bushes, watching her. The water was dirty—empty bottles, tin cans, and all kinds of rubbish floated along—but she did not quite care. He folded his arms, smiling, as he observed her in amusement. A girl who would swim alone in such a filthy river was unusual. Unconventional. Brave, perhaps.

A vague misgiving, however, began to gnaw at him when he remembered the stories he had heard about crocodiles in the river. Ah Pui had once warned the regular patrons at the coffee shop of these reptiles, recounting in his typical dramatic fashion how he had seen one basking in the sun on the riverbank; he had stretched his arms wide as he described a two-metre-long creature to the wide-eyed, awe-struck children whose spoons of chicken rice were left suspended in mid-air.

He tried to shake off these thoughts. No, Ah Pui must have been exaggerating. If it were true, Ah Pui would not have dared to go for a swim there. But still, he hastily came out from behind the bushes, calling out to Snow as he did so. Realizing he had been watching her, she threw a stone at him. 'How dare you hide and watch me!' she rebuked.

From time to time, they saw otters in the river. She taught him to play the harmonica, and he helped her with her schoolwork as she prepared for the GCE 'O' level examinations. She learnt that he had done well in his 'O' level exams, that his mind was sharp, and he was proficient in his academic work. Whenever she encouraged him to pursue his studies, however, he fell silent.

She also learnt that he avoided talking about his family; while he spoke fondly of his two elder sisters, especially his Dai Kah Jie, he would change the subject when she asked about his parents. This much she could gather—that his Ba did not live with them, and that his Ma did not talk much to him. He deflected her questions about the long scar on his arm as well, looking away and giving vague replies about fighting when he was younger.

One afternoon in June 1976, Yang sat waiting by the river. He looked at his watch. Snow would normally have arrived much earlier. It was, moreover, the school holidays, so she could not have been delayed in school. Not having seen her since they last met three weeks ago, a mixture of disappointment and unease sat on his furrowed brow. Could something have happened to her? Could she have forgotten? Or, perhaps, she simply did not wish to continue seeing him, to continue meeting at the river.

When afternoon gave way to evening, he got up. Not without some hesitation, he headed in the direction of her family's provision shop. He did not want to seem presumptuous in making an appearance at her shop if she no longer wished to keep up their friendship; nevertheless, he would be ill at ease if he did not at least see her.

Steeling himself, he strode towards the shop.

From a distance, the provision shop looked much more disorganized than it usually was. Boxes of canned food and drinks lay around. The racks outside the shop, which used to hold neatly arranged tins of biscuits, now had just a few tins perched haphazardly on random shelves. His breathing quickened along with his footsteps.

He stepped inside. The place was in disarray. The counter where Nenek normally sat was empty. His mind reeled and his heart froze in his chest. Frantically, he craned his neck; peered down the first aisle. He could see neither Snow nor her family there. He moved towards the second aisle. Still no sign of her. He almost ran into the third aisle. Just as he did so, someone walked out from the aisle. There was a bump of two bodies, and cans of baked beans fell to the floor. The sound of the metal cans clanging onto the cement floor pulled his gaze downwards, then in all directions along with the chaotic rolling of the little barrels of food. He looked up.

Stupefied, she stared at the tins strewn on the floor, after which she looked up at him. He was almost panting, trickles of perspiration on his face which exuded relief and concern in equal measure.

She wanted to smile at the sight of this familiar face she had grown so fond of; at the warm presence of the person she had longed to see so sorely during the past several turbulent weeks; at the affectionate gaze which at this moment brought so deep a comfort that her heart ached in both solace and sorrow.

His gaze not lifting from her, he spoke tenderly, 'What happened?'

Two simple words. They were just two simple words. *What happened*. Yet, why did they call forth the disobedient tears which would not retreat?

He stood there patiently when she did not answer, did not know how to answer. He stooped to pick up the cans of baked beans, placing them back on the shelf.

Again, he asked gently as he stacked the cans, 'Where's your Ma and Nenek?'

'Upstairs … too sad … Ba … heart attack …' her words fell out in fragments, like mismatched pieces of jigsaw unable to form a coherent picture.

He listened intently, then looked around the shop again.

'Heart attack? Your Ba?'

She nodded, looking down.

With a monumental effort, she pushed the words out and heard them almost as if uttered by someone else.

'He's gone.'

Chapter 17

Nenek pulled at the strings of her waist hem. Her once-fitting pants now hung loose upon the wrinkled skin of her hips. How did you eat when, each time you sat at the table, you remembered that your son would never eat with you again? She looked wearily at the grey-haired old woman staring back at her in the mirror. She was too old. Too old for such heartache. He was only 44 years old.

She took a deep breath, then stepped out of her room. Her daughter-in-law was seated on the sofa. Still. Upright. A bleeding heart hidden behind eyes which could not see. A stiff, unwomanly face belying the tender, wounded heart of a woman who had just lost her husband.

She managed a slight turn of her head when she heard the door open. 'Ma,' she said quietly. She stood up; held her hand out to her late husband's mother.

Nenek took her hand; held it in hers. Her heart cracked again, and the tears barged into the small space between two heartbroken women. With the other hand, Su Mei wiped the tears from Nenek's face. They both knew that going down to the shop would take all the strength they could muster; two weeks had passed with a few failed attempts to step out. Yet, they knew that it had been hard on Snow, having to manage the shop on her own. The remnants of their motherly heartbeat nudged them to step out. To step up.

With slow, heavy steps, they walked hand in hand towards the shop. From a distance, Nenek saw the outline of a man stooping to lift a box, then carrying it into the shop. For a moment, her breath stopped and her grip on Su Mei's hand tightened. Could it be? How could it be?

The man now walked out of the shop, this time with her granddaughter beside him. Seeing the two older women approaching, they came forward. Snow reached out to her mother and Nenek, who now saw that it was a young man standing beside her granddaughter, not her son.

The young man greeted them with a nod. Yes, Snow had told them. This young man had been coming to help her out at the shop. The young man whose father had delivered Pepsi bottles to their shop in the kampong many years back, and whom a recent outpouring of rain from the heavens above had sent here, in search of shelter. A crossing of paths once again.

Nenek took her usual seat at the front counter, while Su Mei went to the back. Snow arranged the newly arrived stock on the shelves, her hair slightly dishevelled, her face pale, and her eyes glazed, while Yang carried the heavy boxes in, slit them open with a pen knife, and passed the cans of food and drink to her.

From where she was seated, Nenek watched the young man as he lifted another box, the sweat glistening on his arms. It was not her son, but perhaps, the heavens, too, had remnants of a living heartbeat, vestiges of compassion's rhythms, which sent this young man to them in this time of need.

As the weeks wore on, a resigned rhythm settled into life at the provision shop.

Su Mei and Nenek took care of the shop while Snow was at school. When she got home, she took over, with the two older women going upstairs to take rest, before resuming the daily chores of cooking, washing, cleaning, and ironing. When there was a paucity of customers, Snow would do her schoolwork at the shop.

On most days, Yang would be there, helping in whatever way he could. There was a short circuit one evening which threw the entire place into darkness. One of the ceiling lights had blown up. He wanted to climb the ladder to fix it, but Snow insisted that she be the one to do so, if he would only teach her how to.

At the end of each week, Su Mei would press into his hands a portion of the shop's modest earnings. If he resisted, he would find a small amount of money in his bag when he got home. Many a time, she would gently squeeze his arm, saying 'thank you' as she did so. He would look at her unseeing eyes and wonder what her life, Snow's life, would have been like if she had not been so badly burned.

On the days he helped Snow, he could not work at the coffee shop. Gradually, as his absence at the coffee shop became more frequent, a brother of one of the stallholders began taking over his duties there, in spite of Ah Pui's attempts to retain his position for him. The coffee shop's business was brisk, and the work had to be done by someone.

Yang had, in effect, lost his job.

Chapter 18

On a warm August night, Yang walked down the busy streets of Chinatown, a hundred pirated cassettes in the large haversack on his back. He had obtained these cassettes from Long Kor, who worked as a hawker during the day and peddled these cassettes in the night.

He pulled his wallet from his pocket, counting the few notes left. While Snow's family shared their earnings with him, he did not want to impose on their family financially. His Ma naturally had no knowledge that he had lost his job at the coffee shop. Neither did Dai Kah Jie. He and Dai Kah Jie shouldered equal parts of their household's financial needs, and he could not—must not—add to her already tough lot of selling vegetables at the market, in addition to having to take care of their mother and the house.

The bustling lanes of Temple Street and Pagoda Street in Chinatown presented ample opportunity to hawk his cassettes. He knew it was hostile gangster territory, but he had to take the risk. He did not know what compelled him to help Snow—was this what they called love? Was he in love with her? He did not know. He only knew that his heart ached when he looked upon the tiredness of her face, the helplessness in her eyes. She had to take care of her mother, her Nenek, and the shop. She had to study. The GCE 'O' level exams were just round the corner. He had to help her.

And yet, persisting down this road could get him into conflict with rival gangs, trouble which might spill over to hurt her. Those gangsters might create a scene at the provision shop. And now his heart ached even more acutely, for he was no longer sure whether he was helping her, or whether he was making her vulnerable to being hurt. A convoluted well of emotions rose, riding on a voice which seemed to mock him. *You are a gangster. A nobody. What makes you think you are worthy of helping her, of being someone special to her?*

He stopped in his tracks; closed his eyes; clenched his fists. Yes, perhaps he should stay away from her. The thought of the shop being overturned and ransacked, or worse still, of aggressive men intimidating her, seared through his entire body. Yet, if he did not help her tide through this difficult time, who would? Her father had been the only man in their household, and he had gone so suddenly. Snow, her mother, and grandmother would probably find their footing in time, but that was it—they needed time.

Perhaps all he was meant to do was to buy them time, to see her through her upcoming examinations, to keep the shop up and running till then. In doing so, he was, in fact, buying himself time as well—time with her. Once she cleared her exams, his job would be done, and he would distance himself from her. In the meantime, he had to be very careful in covering his tracks.

With renewed resolve, he strode towards Temple Street. He set up his makeshift stall there, displaying his cassettes beside another street stall selling durians, not far from the Sri Mariamman Temple.

'Lelong! Lelong! Sale! Sale!' he called out to the throngs of shoppers and pedestrians. Some came over to browse, and soon sales picked up. Within an hour, he had sold dozens of cassettes.

From the corner of his eye, he noticed two men in blue walking into the street.

'Police coming! Quick! Run!' the durian seller who, like Yang, did not have a license, shouted out to him.

Deftly, he shoved the unsold cassettes into his haversack and folded the flimsy wooden table on which he displayed his wares. Seeing the durian seller struggling to pack the thorny fruits into sacks, Yang hastily helped the man. The two of them ran, pushing the cart of durians.

The two policemen caught sight of them running and gave chase with shouts of 'Stop there!' Luckily for them, the thick crowds made their escape possible. Adroitly, they weaved through the human traffic till the policemen lost their trail.

Later, when he reached the safety of his block, Yang took out his wallet. He broke into a boyish smile—he had earned enough to last a few weeks.

One afternoon in September, he arrived at the shop later than usual. Snow was taken aback when he finally hobbled in—his face and arms were covered in bruises, his left eye swollen. He simply put his bag down and got to work, taking stock of wares. When she asked him what had happened, he did not reply. Nor did he meet her gaze. It was only after a long silence that he uttered two words, 'I'm fine.' With that, he carried on with his chores, avoiding her.

As she watched his sullen, wounded figure, it dawned on her that there was so much about him she did not know.

And it seemed as though he did not wish for her to know. He had been acting peculiar in recent weeks—coming and going at odd, unpredictable hours, appearing one day, and not appearing the next, often looking over his shoulders to see if anyone had been tailing him—in a demeanour that was almost surreptitious, it seemed.

His presence in her time of need, of grief, had been a cherished source of comfort; a warm companionship she looked forward to each day. She and her family might not have made it through the past months without his help. More than that, she wondered if her fondness of him went beyond that of friendship. There had been the occasional night when, after they had closed the shop, they had sat on the void deck outside, chatting. She had dozed off, and when she opened her eyes, she realized she had been leaning against his shoulder. The sour-sweet, musky scent of his sweat-laced T-shirt lingered in her senses, its distinct odour taking her back to the time of their first encounter, when this very same scent had lingered on her own skin after she had worn his shirt.

She could not focus on her schoolwork on the days he did not show up. Once, when he finally walked into the shop after seven long days, she felt a choking tightness in her chest which she could not quite describe, other than that it was tender yet biting. He had gazed at her so tenderly and affectionately—as if his eyes were telling her, *I have missed you very much too*—yet he had kept his distance, not uttering a word. It was as if he cared deeply for her, but was determined to remain detached.

Now, as she beheld his sad, sunken eyes nestled amid the distended swells of bruised eyelids, so did a sharp pain nestle amid the swells of her confounded heart, and all she could do was to go about her work in the sombre companionship of his silent presence.

Chapter 19

The GCE 'O' level examinations came and went. The year was drawing to a close, and on a cool, wet morning in December, Snow's Nenek told her that their relatives from Indonesia had asked them to relocate to Bandung. Snow knew that her Nenek was from Bandung. Her father had been born there. In 1948, after WWII, at the age of 16, he had moved to Singapore with his parents and had settled down here, where he met her mother.

In a month or two, Nenek's younger brother and his son would be coming to Singapore to assist in their relocation.

She understood—how could they carry on running the shop like this? She was too young, her Nenek was too old, and her mother was blind. Her mother's parents—her maternal grandparents—had already passed on, and her mother's only sister had a family of her own to take care of.

What would happen to their shop? she asked. It would have to be sold, her Nenek replied.

She remained pensive. The semblance of a related question, an almost clandestine one which she could not voice out to

Nenek, nor to anyone else, but which grew in urgency as she envisioned an oblique future in a new land, gradually surfaced from the turbulence of her thoughts: what would happen to Yang? What would happen to their … their what? Their relationship? What relationship was it anyway? He was not her boyfriend. He had never made his feelings towards her clear. Perhaps it had just been childish infatuation on her part all along. Yet, why had he gone out of his way to help her if he did not see their friendship, their relationship, as something special to him? Was he merely helping a friend in need?

Sensing the emotional disquiet in her granddaughter, Nenek placed her hand on Snow's cheek. With an affectionate smile, she said, 'I know. He's good, that young man. He's been kind to us.'

Taken aback, Snow looked up at Nenek, who nodded, 'You're still young. Maybe in future, both of you can meet again.'

Snow tried to smile but couldn't. Nenek continued, 'Talk to him. He will understand. We cannot go on burdening him like that. He's still young. He must create a future for himself, you understand?'

That afternoon, Snow waited for Yang to turn up at the shop. The afternoon light gently gave way to the kiss of the dusk, a kiss which tarried upon the face of the earth till it could not but bid a weary goodnight.

A vexed pair of hands pulled hard on the shutters, almost slamming it onto the cement floor. What was wrong with him? He was supposed to come today. He said he would. Was not a man only as good as his word? Exasperation creased her face, its energy slamming her eyelids shut, squeezing them tightly. No. Perhaps the question should not have been about him, but about her. Yes. What was wrong with her? Why had she become so needy of him? In every way shy of a verbal confirmation—his helping her at the shop, the companionship they had shared, the tenderness in his voice and eyes—he had seemed to convey his affections for her. Yet, he always held back. He held back from her not just his proclamation of love, but his entire life. She did not know what he did when he was not at the shop; she did not know what his plans for the future were; she had not seen his family, nor the place where he lived.

The copious, harried energy that had been knocking about inside finally let itself free in her long, tired breath. She sat on the cement floor with her back against the metal shutters, in the same way she had sat with him by her side numerous times. What did it matter anyway? In a month or two, she would be gone from his life. She would have to begin a new life in a new country. There would be no more provision shop, no more working alongside him, no more sitting alongside him at the river, no more waiting in vain for him to turn up. Perhaps, it was better this way. It would be easier to say goodbye.

Yes, perhaps that was all that was left for her to do. To say goodbye.

Chapter 20

Three days later, she was at the counter talking to a customer when he walked in. He gave a slight smile as he caught sight of her, his gaze resting on her, tarrying as if beholding one dearly missed.

She saw him; there came the familiar tightening in her chest that was warm and acrid all at once. With a deliberate turn back towards the customer, she paid him no heed.

He put his bag down; looked around. It had been over a week since his last visit. He had not forgotten what he had told her, that he was supposed to have come three days ago. His non-appearance was probably the reason behind her cold demeanour, he thought. But how was he to explain that he was being trailed by men from rival gangs? That the more he longed to come and see her, the deeper became the fear that he would bring harm upon her, and the more he had to resist proximity? That when he started helping her, he had already known that his job would be done once she completed her exams.

How was he to tell her that he was no good for her, that as things were, he did not have what it took to give her a safe, decent future?

As he lifted the heavy boxes of canned drinks from the storeroom, the heaviness in his heart would not lift. Perhaps, tonight, when they closed the shop, he ought to tell her that he would not be coming anymore. Would he be able to say that to her? His eyes squeezed shut; his hands clenched the edge of the box he was carrying. That this might be the last day he would see her sent a pain shooting through his body like arrows of merciless fire.

In this manner, the silent, conflicted afternoon wore on, looking upon two souls whose burning masculine energy and chilly feminine resolve belied two hearts indistinguishable in their ache.

When night fell and the shop had emptied itself of customers, he finally stole a glance at her. She was unusually quiet, as if something were bothering her. Was today not the best time to say goodbye, he wondered, not without a surge of gladness, and, if so, perhaps he could savour the sweetness of their bond a little longer? He shook his head. No. He must not waver. The time the shop closed tonight would be the time he must bid her farewell.

She caught sight of his glance from the corner of her eye but pretended not to notice. She knew he was under the impression that she was angry at his no-show three days ago. Like him, she had deliberately kept her distance. Maybe, just maybe, this distance would make it easier to tell him that the shop would soon be sold, that she would soon leave the country.

Not knowing where to direct his restless energy, he picked up two empty cardboard cartons and carried these outside.

As he was about to place the cartons outside, he sensed the presence of hostile, watchful eyes. He spun around. There, just fifty meters away, stood three men.

His heart lurched. His worst fears had come true. They had finally tracked him down to the shop.

Dropping the cardboard, he looked quickly over his shoulder to make sure that she was safe inside before racing towards them.

'Don't make trouble for the shop,' he panted as he stood facing them. In all the brawls he had been through, till today, fear was never an issue. What was there to lose other than his small life, which was not worth very much anyway? Fear not for himself, but for her safety. Steeling himself, he glared at their leader. 'We settle this, man to man. Somewhere else, not here.'

The bald leader stared back at him, then nodded.

Back at the shop, Snow heard the sound of cardboard being thrown to the ground. When Yang did not return, she went out to take a look, only to see his back from a distance, walking away with three large men. They were walking in the direction of the river. Hurriedly, she pulled down the shutters and ran after them.

As she neared the river, the sounds of punches accompanied by angry shouts of pain grew louder. She crouched behind a row of shrubs, heart thumping. Carefully, she raised herself slightly, knees bent, so as to catch a glimpse of the scuffle.

She gasped. Yang, bruised and bleeding from the nose, was fighting three men, one against three. She sprung back behind the shrubs, recalling the time when he had come to the shop bruised all over, but had refused to speak about it.

There came a sudden, loud thud. She peered from the shrubs—he had fallen to the ground, panting and bleeding.

A ball of fury began swirling inside her, amassing energy, growing in speed, till she gave a loud cry, grabbed a fallen branch and charged towards the three men, who looked astonished at the sudden appearance of a girl from behind the shrubs. Yang, still on the ground, turned around and held his breath when he saw her charging towards his assailants.

With all her might, she swung the branch at the bald man. He caught it with his hand; wrenched it out of her hand. The force propelled her backward, causing her to lose her balance and fall to the ground. Yang, stunned initially by her sudden appearance, jumped back onto his feet, and placed himself between the men and her, his arms outstretched the way one used one's body to protect a loved one.

'Leave her alone!' he growled.

The bald man looked from the wounded opponent in front of him to the young lady glowering at him from where she lay on the ground. Never before had a young lady charged at him so fearlessly. A glint of respect crept into his eyes, and he burst out in a guffaw. Looking at Yang, he pointed towards the young lady; gave a thumbs up. Then he turned towards her, saying, 'Tell your man to stop selling his cassettes in my area.'

He signalled his men to leave, and they walked off.

When they had left, Yang helped Snow to her feet. 'What are you doing here? They could have hurt you. Or ... even worse ...' As these words tumbled out in vehemence, he realized he had been overcome with panic, with fear, when she fell to the ground, for the two men could have pinned him down while their leader did unthinkable things to her.

'What am I doing here?' she retorted, 'Shouldn't I be asking you? You disappear from the shop, and I find you here, beaten and bleeding! What was I to do? Watch you being punched and kicked all over?'

They stood facing each other, the space between their hearts choked with loud, angry breaths. She beheld his wounded face, his averted gaze which did not dare meet hers, his bruised body which had stood fearlessly between her and their aggressors.

'I don't know you,' she blurted out, a tear streaming down her face. 'I … I am so fond of you, but I don't know anything about you! Who are you really, Lee Yang? Who are you? Why are you hiding everything from me?'

Her anguished words shot through him like splinters of ember. He stared at her soft face, at those eyes he had longed to caress, at the lips he had longed to kiss, at the body he had longed to touch. His breathing quickened, his mind began spinning, and a dark being burst forth from some murky, hidden depths.

Gripping her shoulders, he hissed, 'You wanna know who I am? You saw for yourself today!' His voice grew louder. 'This is who I am! A lousy gangster, you understand?'

With that, he pressed his lips forcefully against hers as he clutched the fabric of her blouse, clothing which, in his fantasies, he had lifted so gently to reveal her body. He did not want to lose her—no, he needed her and desired her so badly that he was terrified of losing her, of losing her smile, her touch, her warmth, and her respect; yet the only way to love her, to protect her, was to keep her away from him; and in the end they had come to this, to the revelation of who he truly was, to the darkness in his life which he had hoped for her never to see; and with all the strength he could muster he stopped himself from tearing her clothes off, stopped his lips from forcing themselves onto hers, and he tore himself away from her, slumping onto the ground.

It was the only thing he could do to salvage the last shreds of respect she might have had for him.

He sat panting on the ground, not daring to look at her. What had he just done? Didn't he just prove that he was indeed a vagabond, that he should have stayed away from her right from the start?

She stood bewildered, rooted to the ground, flushed and breathless, not knowing what to think. He had just kissed her. In her girlish daydreams she had imagined what the moment of her first kiss would be like; she had imagined how her heart would leap in joy, how the night sky would light up in starry romance. She had not imagined that it would be such a bittersweet moment; that heartache would kick romance out of the door.

With his words, he had finally revealed what he had been hiding from her. Was the man before her now no longer the same man she had known before? Perhaps it did not matter anymore.

With his kiss, he had finally revealed his feelings for her. She no longer had to live in the unbearable state of guessing and not knowing, hoping, and yet doubting.

And knowing this now was perhaps the most precious, and the cruellest, parting gift she could have hoped for.

She said quietly to his huddled figure, 'I'm going to Bandung. Next month. We are going to sell the shop. Going to live in Bandung. My Nenek's relatives are there.'

He listened without looking at her. He wanted to tell her how much she had brought into his life, but the words would not come, as though those words, once spoken, would soften the fraught distance now between them, and would make it more difficult for him to let her leave.

He nodded in acknowledgment of what she had just told him. He longed to have one last look at her, to have her face burned into his memory like the songs on his cassettes. Yet, he could not look at her. He had to let her go. He had never felt so afraid of losing someone; had never been so terrified that he would break down and cry like a coward.

And he had never felt so fearful of himself; of what he had almost done to her; of what he was capable of doing to her.

As she looked at him, the ache inside her continued unabated. She waited for him to say something. When he did not, she said quietly through the tears, 'Thank you. For helping me. I will always remember you. Take care of yourself.'

She took one final look at him, then turned and walked away slowly, heavily.

His eyes squeezed shut, he listened to her familiar footfall fading into the night wind. Finally, he turned in her direction; watched her distant figure slipping away from his life. For the first time in his adult life, his vision began to blur from the wetness in his eyes, and his breathing constricted from the excruciating tightness in his chest.

He turned back towards the sounds of the water, continuing to sit there, looking out over the dark river. Perhaps, he was indeed not meant to get too close to her, for the fiery sun would ravage the most pristine sea of snow, unless it merely gazed on it from a distance.

For a moment, he saw again his father walking out of their flat—to get a better job elsewhere, leaving them so as to provide for them. A feeling of being closer to his father than he had ever been stung him; for perhaps all that his father had done, and all that he was now doing, was learning how to be a man.

Chapter 21

A month later.

She pulled the small cassette player from her bag as she sat on the damp grass of the riverbank. The following day, on 1 February 1977, she would be leaving Singapore. She did not know when, or if, she would be coming back.

She had not seen Yang since the day of the fight. One morning a week ago, she had found a small parcel, with her name on it, left at the provision shop. He had left it there—she recognized his handwriting. Inside, she found a small cassette player and a cassette with nothing on its cover.

This cassette she now took out, slotting it into the player. Background noise was all there was at first, similar to the sounds she could hear from the edge of the river. After a minute though, squeaks became discernible, and as she listened intently, a small, sad smile crept onto her face.

The otters. The sounds of the river. He had given her a special gift—a gift of the water.

Early morning showers had bequeathed a sparkling field of tiny raindrops which hung from the leaves all around, like a thousand little beads of water diamonds, holding and reflecting glints of the sun in a splendid dance of light.

A lone grey heron perched on a nearby rock. She looked out over the river to the handkerchief trees in the distance. A light breeze was nuzzling the green tassels, the handkerchiefs, so that they fluttered and tugged at the branch holding them back, as if wanting to reach out, to offer the comfort of a soft touch, but were yet bound to the unmoving branches where they were meant to be.

The solitary sun, in all his fiery resplendence and majesty, sat unaccompanied in the vast sky, gazing from a distance at the river as she swayed along. Each a solo dance. The river, in all her beauty and tenacity, weaved her own, long way across the earth towards the ocean. The sun and the river, thus, continued their dialectical discourse, through which emerged the abundance of the earth.

As she sat there for the last time this afternoon, the sun seemed to her to be a forlorn sun. And the river, a lonely river.

Part Three

Earth

Light and life gifted by the sun
Yet scars are overflowing
Washing the parched land
Into brave, lonely seas
Earth, poisoned abundance
Cries out in song

***

1986

Chapter 22

The sky turned white. Screams rang through the clouds of concrete dust. Six storeys of stone fell to the earth with a loud *'boom'*, cascading down, bringing with them shattered glass and shattered lives. On the ground all around, people were screaming and fleeing, blinded by the white ash. In barely a minute, the building had become a heap of rubble, a massive tomb in which lay the bodies of people, some still alive.

The Lian Yak Building along Serangoon Road, which had housed the Hotel New World, along with a branch of the Industrial and Commercial Bank, and a nightclub, had been reduced to naught.

Ten minutes later, two fire engines from the Singapore Fire Service arrived. The firefighters disembarked in haste, only to behold a sight they had never encountered before. For a moment they stood there, stunned by the scale of the disaster, unsure of what they should do; for they were trained to fight fires and to save people from fires, but none of them had ever stood in the face of such a large building collapse.

Lee Yang, who had arrived in the second fire engine, stood among his fellow firefighters. Beside him stood Alif, his childhood kampong friend and fellow officer in the fire service.

'There's someone trapped here!'

A group of men called out to the firefighters, for they had seen the bloodied arm of a person protruding from the debris. Dozens of untrained civilians were at the collapse site, trying to help in the rescue effort. Together with these volunteers, Yang and his team hurriedly removed the debris with their hands and freed the trapped man who, to their relief, was still alive. They found another survivor, a female tourist, near the surface of the rubble, and managed to pull her out to safety.

Soon, the police, the Singapore Armed Forces, the Civil Defence Force, and the medical services were there. The area was cordoned off, and civilians were asked to leave the site. Ministers began to arrive, as did journalists.

The entire nation watched as the rescuers raced against time to search for survivors of the worst building collapse in the country's history.

The rescuers could hear faint cries of help from a woman buried not far below the surface of the rubble, but they could not see her. She was probably injured, with little oxygen and no water. They had to reach her quickly.

With their hands, Yang, Alif, and their fire team pulled away pieces of debris near the woman's location. As with all the fire breakouts they had been through together, there was a sense of urgency, an impulse to do what it took to save a life; but they knew they had to be as careful as they were anxious, for the collapsed structure was unstable, and could shift or collapse further at any moment. Victims beneath, who were still alive, could then be crushed.

When they had carefully removed enough debris to peer inside, they could see the woman's feet about six metres away. The only way to reach her was for them to dig through the wreckage to pull her out.

'I'll go,' Alif told Yang.

Yang placed his hands on Alif's shoulders and nodded, as they exchanged a look of understanding and friendship, a gesture as brief as it was deep. There was no time to lose. Soon, Alif and Yusoff, one of their teammates, were inching their way into the rubble, crawling slowly and carefully so as not to destabilize the structure. Yang watched as Alif and Yusoff made painstaking progress, ready to go forward any time should any of the beams give way and collapse on his friends and teammates.

He and Alif had been through many fires together, since they joined the fire service nine years ago. After Snow left, he had stopped selling cassettes. Emptiness, cloaked in despondency, sat on his days and nights. A burning desire to put his gangster days behind gripped him. It was Alif who had suggested that they join the fire service together. 'Last time, you fight people. Now, we fight fire. Save people,' Alif had said.

Once, not long after they had become firefighters, there was a child trapped in a shophouse fire. Yang had dashed in to grab the child and was running out of the shophouse, when a beam fell on him, pinning him to the ground. Alif, who had been outside, trying to douse the flames, had immediately dived forward to lift the beam, freeing him and the child. They had managed to escape from the blaze with just mild injuries.

Now, as Alif and Yusoff edged further into the collapsed structure, Yang found himself fearing for their safety. Yet, this was what they were called to do. Trepidation accompanied them each time they approached a fire, but when they saw someone trapped, shouting for help, they knew they had to do what it took to save a person who might, otherwise, die. At times, when they sat recovering in one another's company after a fire, they did wonder, did look back at their decision to join the fire service; had they known what the job truly entailed, would they have signed on the dotted lines? Would they have decided to risk paying the ransom for another life with their own? And yet, disaster rescue had now become their life; it defined who they were, an identity much more inexplicable than a call of duty.

A sudden creak of the concrete slabs jolted everyone. 'The beams are shifting!' one of his men shouted. Everyone held their breath.

'Alif! Stop! Keep still!' Yang shouted into the tunnel.

Alif, panting from the tunnelling and the lack of oxygen, kept still. There was more creaking as the top of the collapsed structure heaved like a yawning giant they had awakened. A large concrete slab broke in two. One of the broken halves cascaded down along the side of the heap.

Heart racing, Yang frantically shone a torch towards Alif's location in the tunnel.

'Alif!'

'We're okay!' came Alif's reply.

A collective sigh of relief emanated from all around. They waited for a few minutes. When the groans of the structure quietened, Alif and Yusoff resumed their tunnelling.

Over two hours later, the two firemen finally emerged from the tunnel, covered in concrete dust. They had pulled the woman to the entrance to the tunnel, where she was lifted onto a stretcher, injured and mildly delirious, but alive. Paramedics rushed her to an awaiting Air Force helicopter which airlifted her to the Singapore General Hospital.

Elated, everyone at the site cheered. Perhaps nothing in this world could be compared to the joy of knowing that a life had been saved.

Soon after, rescue operations focused on cutting and lifting concrete slabs from the top of the rubble in order to reach survivors. A hundred-ton crane was brought in for this cut-and-lift approach. A high-level committee was convened to coordinate the rescue effort which involved the fire service, the police, the military, and the civil defence force.

On the ground, rescue personnel became increasingly concerned that the cut-and-lift method could endanger the survivors still trapped inside. The heavy machinery, compounded by the destabilizing effect of cutting and lifting large pieces of concrete, could cause massive, localized collapse of the structure.

As the night wore on, the walls that had once enfolded the lives of people—their livelihoods and leisure, their surreptitiousness and secrets, their camaraderie and companionships—continued to moan as towering metal structures cut into the concrete, parts of which were lifted, and parts of which crumbled back into the floundering heap.

For many hours, all they uncovered were dead bodies.

Chapter 23

The television screen was filled with the desperation of people huddled together. Their sobs broke the hearts of all in the country who were watching the unfolding of events. Through the despair in their eyes, glimmers of hope still shone through; perhaps their loved ones were still alive, buried beneath the debris but still breathing; waiting, hoping for rescuers to reach them. The officials and rescuers had assured them, had assured the entire nation, had they not? That no effort was being spared to rescue those buried under the monstrous mess. Deep in the belly of the collapsed, concrete cavern, lay living, breathing souls who could perhaps be pulled from the fingers of death by another living, breathing soul brave enough to crawl in to reach them.

Snow sat in front of the television, appalled by the unbelievable collapse of Hotel New World, saddened by the distress of families and relatives gathered at the site. As the news station brought updates of the disaster through the day and night, she joined in the muffled cheers of neighbours when someone was pulled out alive, and sat despondently when someone was pulled out, dead.

At some point during the night, or in the early hours of the morning—for even time seemed to hold its breath as the minutes and hours now listened to the heartbeat of the rescue—she jolted from where she had been lying on the sofa; sprang towards the television, touching the screen as if hoping to find a 'rewind' button.

Was that him? Had she seen whom she thought she had seen? The camera had momentarily trained on the rescuers at the site of the collapse, and she had caught a fleeting glimpse of a face she had been so fond of before she left the country. Nine years. They had lost contact for nine years, the first few of which she had pined for his friendship, his companionship. His love.

She made a phone call to her friend Meiyun who, while berating her for calling at such an unearthly hour, was nevertheless happy to hear the voice of a friend who had been away for such a long time. Snow asked Meiyun if she knew what Yang and Ah Pui were doing now. Meiyun had lost touch with them in recent years, but recalled that not too long after Snow had left Singapore, Yang had joined the fire service, and that he worked and studied at the same time.

Her thoughts raced as she put down the phone. Was that firefighter really him? There was only one way to find out.

The rays of the morning sun landed softly on the weary, resolute faces of the rescuers who had worked through the night. They had managed to save a few more, but with the passing of each minute, each hour, they knew that those still buried were slipping away.

Behind the cordon, people continued to gather—concerned owners and workers of nearby establishments, onlookers from all over the island, volunteers waiting for updates to convey to relatives of victims housed at a coffee shop in the vicinity.

Snow stood among the crowd behind the cordon. She could not see any of the rescuers clearly, for they were mostly at the back of the site. There was a sudden flurry of activity among the rescuers. A body had just been found. The rescuers placed the body on a stretcher, covered it with a piece of cloth, and carried it away. Snow craned her neck to catch sight of these rescuers, but she did not recognize any of them.

She wandered to the coffee shop where the next of kin were waiting, where the anguish she had seen on screen came alive. People young and old sat wordlessly on stools, their silence belying the agony, the anxiety written on their faces and flowing through their eyes.

A police officer strode in, his eyes downcast. He looked at a slip of paper in his hand, then spoke in hushed tones to a Red Cross volunteer there. The volunteer pointed discreetly to an elderly woman seated at a corner. The police officer approached the grey-haired woman, gently putting his hand on her shoulder. She gazed up at his face from where she was seated. Her chest began to heave. Those around her held on to her as her body went limp; others burst out in sobs at the news of one more death, at the extinguishing of one more thread of hope.

Snow found herself unable to breathe. She stumbled out of the coffee shop—she had to leave the place. She had not been able to catch a glimpse of him, but the pain she had just encountered was too much to bear.

She staggered away in a daze. Perhaps, when she could pull herself together, she would come again later.

Chapter 24

On the second day of the rescue operation, Yang gathered his team of firefighters to convey the instructions he had just received from his chief. There was to be a change in the mode of rescue.

Engineers working on tunnelling works for the Mass Rapid Transit (MRT) train system had studied the building plans, and advised that there could be survivors trapped in the basement carpark of the building, deep beneath the rubble. The concrete walls of the basement carpark could have withstood the collapse, leaving pockets of space where there could be survivors. Continued lifting of the wreckage from the top could destabilize the structure, leading to further collapse which would endanger the possible survivors in the basement.

Their first priority was to try to ascertain if there were indeed survivors in the basement. Singapore Civil Defence Force (SCDF) officers placed sound amplifying equipment from life detector devices at various locations. They spoke through a loudhailer to ask any possible survivors to knock lightly on the walls.

Everyone fell silent as the civil defence officers listened intently for sounds of life. After a few minutes, they picked up sounds of knocking. Yes, there were people trapped far below. And they were still alive.

The rescuers sprang into action. Together with the tunnelling experts, the firefighters and the civil defence personnel prepared to tunnel deep into the wreckage. The building had collapsed into the centre of the basement, which meant that they had to work their way around the edges. To get to the opposite side, they had to skirt the walls of the basement; had to tunnel in a roundabout way. A longer way.

Yang and Alif put on their helmets with torches.

'Let's go,' Alif said to Yang.

With that, they began crawling into the darkness, along with a few other teammates.

Behind the cordon, talk about the tunnelling effort was abuzz among onlookers.

'*Wah!* What if the concrete collapses on the rescuers? So dangerous man!' someone exclaimed.

'Yah, it's so unstable, can collapse any time,' another echoed.

'Maybe the tunnelling experts can shore up the tunnels. Make it safe,' a third said.

'*Aiya*, even then, can still collapse right? So much rubble on top, you know!'

'True. Brave ah, these rescuers!'

Snow stood among the crowd; listened to what was being said. She had recovered somewhat from her traumatic encounter with death in the morning, had come back here in the afternoon.

Without warning, concrete blocks slid off the massive, mangled heap as the unsteady structure tremored. The rescuers around the rubble scrambled away from the falling stones amid shouts to one another.

She stared, horrified, at the cascading concrete. Was Yang among the rescuers now tunnelling in the wreckage? She did not know, but as she gazed at the monstrosity in the distance, there was a churn in her stomach she could not fully understand. What if it were really him that she had seen on TV? The moment she had seen him on screen had been an exhilarating one, for had she not harboured hopes of seeing him again when she decided to come back to Singapore? And had she not wondered how she was going to find him?

Yet, standing in the face of this harrowing disaster, she now fervently wished that she had been mistaken, that he was not among those who, in order to save another, were going into the depths of the earth themselves.

Yang pulled himself forward inch by inch into the treacherous belly of the wreckage, the drops of perspiration falling onto the wood, metal, and earth beneath him. The beams above him grunted in acknowledgment of his intrusion.

In all his years as a firefighter, he had never had to tunnel in such a manner into such colossal ruins. His body felt trapped—he could barely lift his elbow sideways—and all around him unsteady structures threatened to crumble any time. It took hours just to advance a few meters. Even breathing was difficult in the narrow, dusty tunnel. He had to cut through pipes or wood blocking the way using a small blade. His muscles ached from his body being fettered in narrow confines, from having to exert within the little space he had to drag himself forward in the dark tunnel, where the only light was the one on his helmet.

After what seemed like hours of arduous, strenuous crawling, he could finally see the basement carpark. He tried to steady his breathing as he surveyed the area lit by the torch on his helmet. Under long wooden and metal beams crisscrossed all over, cars lay partially submerged in water. The air reeked of petrol.

Suddenly, there was shuddering all around, as if this earthen creature was lurching in order to belch them out. Generous outpourings of sand and cement showered on Yang and his comrades. Shouts from his fellow firefighters in the tunnel rang out.

'Beams shifting!' he yelled to Alif, who was not far behind in the tunnel.

'Keep still!' Alif shouted back.

Panting, he closed his eyes, lying as still as he could. In that moment, the thought of possibly dying in there seized him. If he were to be buried by an avalanche of concrete, would the world remember him? Would his Ba grieve for him? Would Ma, Dai Kah Jie, and Yee Kah Jie have fond memories of him? Would Snow remember him? Inexplicably, his thoughts went back to the times he had spent with her at the river, at her shop. To the scent of her hair as she fell asleep, and her head rested against his shoulders. To the happiest days of his life.

After a minute, all was still again. Slowly, he opened his eyes. He called out to his comrades to make sure they were all right. Yes, everyone was fine. They climbed into the wider space of the carpark.

Then they heard voices. Voices calling out to them from the far end of the carpark, calling for help. Weak and desperate.

'They're alive,' he said. 'Let's go!'

They had to crawl over the partially submerged cars, but they were met with another obstacle. Water. The place was flooded, and the only way to reach the survivors was to dive underwater.

One by one, they dived into the water, carefully navigating their way through the submerged cars and beams. When they emerged, the voices, which seemed to be coming from behind one of the concrete walls, became louder, clearer. They had to crawl above more cars, dive into more water before reaching the wall. They broke a hole in the wall and shone their torches in.

'They're here! We found them!'

Euphoric shouts erupted from Yang and his team. Still panting from the exertion, they slapped one another's shoulders, beaming. Finally, after risking so much, they had found survivors.

There, in front of them, lay two survivors, a man and a woman. The woman broke into tears when she saw them. She and the man seemed to have suffered slight injuries and were dehydrated but seemed well, otherwise.

Now, the rescuers had to get them out. Fortunately, the duo could move with assistance. They split into two teams, with two firefighters attending to one victim. They began making their way back, exhausted but in high spirits.

A few hours later, the two survivors emerged from the rubble to exuberant applause from everyone at the site. When their rescuers emerged, the cheers from the crowds were equally thunderous. Some of the onlookers handed food, drink, and towels to the rescuers.

From a distance, behind the cordon, Snow's gaze fell on one of the firefighters who had just come out of the wreckage. Her heart raced and her vision began to blur from the wetness in her eyes.

His face was covered in white dust, but it was unmistakable. It was the face that had seen her through the most trying months of her life.

Chapter 25

Rescuers continued to work round the clock in their search for survivors over the next two days. A few more were found alive; many more bodies were unearthed. On 19 March 1986, four days after the collapse, rescue operations were called off. By then, rescuers had pulled out 17 survivors and retrieved 33 bodies.

Prior to the building's collapse, cracks in the walls had appeared, and a toxic carbon monoxide leak had occurred which rendered dozens of the hotel's guests unconscious.

An inquiry commission was set up to investigate the cause of the collapse. The panel would later conclude that the collapse was due to structural defects in the building.

The rescue operation had involved more than 500 personnel from the Singapore Fire Service, Singapore Civil Defence Force, Singapore Armed Forces, Singapore Police Force as well as foreign experts. Many more ordinary citizens volunteered their help and contributions. National awards were bestowed on the individuals and organizations involved in the rescue operations.

Soon after the rescue operations ended, Yang paid a visit to his Ma and Dai Kah Jie, still exhausted from the strain and the trauma of the experience which continued to play out in his mind as he lay on his bed; the scenes of dead bodies seemed ever present, as were the screams and cries for help.

When he first joined the Fire Service, he had moved into the firemen's quarters at the Central Fire Station along Hill Street. Four years ago, after his consistently good performance and the completion of his part-time studies led to his promotion, he moved out of the firemen's quarters into a small flat which he rented on his own behind Cantonment Road, not far from the Central Fire Station.

Dai Kah Jie had been anxious during the days of the rescue; watching the rescue operations on television was nerve-racking, notwithstanding his phone calls to assure her and Ma that he was fine.

When he stepped into their flat, Ma was on the phone, gossiping about a neighbour. A light bulb in the living room had blown, rendering the place partially dark. He climbed onto a chair and began replacing the bulb. Dai Kah Jie walked out from the kitchen where she had been preparing dinner, an affectionate smile lighting up her face as she greeted him.

Ma put an end to her phone gossip session. She addressed him in her characteristic sharp tone of voice, '*Haiya* Yang, why must you have such a dangerous job? You're already 31 years old. All my friends ask me when you're going to get married and I don't know what to tell them!'

'Ma, don't nag at Yang lah. Good enough he's safe and sound,' Dai Kah Jie interjected.

Yang continued to fix the light bulb silently.

'Getting old and not even a girlfriend. Everyday only fighting fires or digging to save other people. Which girl wants to marry a man with such a dangerous job, I ask you? Last time, you like being a gangster. Like to fight people. Now you like to fight fire. What's wrong with you? Why must you fight your whole life?' Ma remarked rhetorically.

Used to his mother's badgering, he climbed down from the chair after finishing with the bulb. Eventually, he said, 'Ma, you said it yourself. Who wants to marry me, right? You should think more for Dai Kah Jie.'

'I never said she cannot marry. She can marry if she wants to,' Ma retorted.

He walked to the toilet to wash his hands before helping Dai Kah Jie to put the food on the table. He then placed an envelope containing a wad of notes in her hands, a routine he had stuck to all these years. Dai Kah Jie had spent her entire life taking care of Ma and the family, and it often pained him to see her bearing the caregiving burden, with the likelihood of finding a companion fading along with her youth.

Later that night, as he lay in bed, his Ma's words came back to him. In his childhood, when his Ba stopped coming home, he had told himself that if ever he did marry, he did not want his marriage to be like that of his parents. Yet in his youth, he had proved as incapable as his Ba and his Ma of not hurting the person he cared for—despite his best efforts, the wound had eventually been inflicted. In his adulthood, he had no desire to venture again into the murky waters of the heart. Occasionally he did think of Snow, and he hoped she was well.

When he decided to join the fire service, after she had left, he had looked up Long Kor at the hawker centre where the latter had a stall selling fried Hokkien noodles. He would no longer help Long Kor pirate his cassettes, no longer fight for the elder brother who had been kind to him. Long Kor encouraged him to join the fire service, adding that he would be getting married and would be giving up the cassette business as well. 'Stop fighting. Start a new life,' Long Kor had advised.

He did start a new life. Yet, after so many years, it seemed that he was still fighting after all. And what it was that he was fighting for, or fighting against, he still did not know.

Chapter 26

Two weeks later, he got a phone call from Ah Pui, suggesting that they meet for dinner. Ah Pui was now managing his family's food business; from the one coffee shop in Kallang, they had expanded to open several more coffee shops around the island. As it was when he was young, Ah Pui's love of food was reflected in his continued rotund physique.

He eyed Yang with a strange look of keen deliberation from across the table.

'Do you know she's back?' he finally asked.

'Who?' Yang replied nonchalantly, poking at the food on his plate with his fork, pretending not to notice Ah Pui's peculiar stare.

'Who? The girl who unglued you when she left the country nine years ago.'

Yang looked up at his friend.

'She came back three months ago. Her family has set up a restaurant in Singapore. They own restaurants in Bandung and other parts of Indonesia. She's running the restaurant here with her cousin.'

Yang resumed poking at his food, but Ah Pui noticed the shallowing of his breathing. He continued, 'She came to the coffee shop to look for me. She saw you, during the hotel collapse. She even went to look for you at the fire station. But you were not there.'

Yang recalled his men telling him that a lady had gone to the station looking for him last week. He had not thought anything of it then.

'So?' Ah Pui needled in his question.

'So what? That was such a long time ago. She's probably married.'

'Uh-uh. She's not. I asked her, for you,' Ah Pui grinned wryly, throwing his friend a look of feigned smugness.

'*Kay-poh* you. A successful businessman, a *towkay*. And so nosy. And thick-skinned too.'

'Yup, I've always been thick-skinned, you know right? And anyway, *towkays* must be like that, if not how to survive?' With Yang not uttering a word, he went on, 'You still think of her, right? So many years and not a girl in your life. Throwing all your energy into your work. Wasn't it because of her that you changed your life? Your gangster days are behind, and now she's back, so there's nothing stopping you now, right?'

Yang said nothing, continuing to stare at his plate. Seeing his friend's rigid silence, Ah Pui sighed and fished out a name card from his wallet. 'Here. The name and address of her restaurant. She asked me to pass it to you.'

Yang took the card from Ah Pui. He stared at the words, 'Nenek's Indonesian Kitchen', printed on it. Below that, 'Salju Hartanto, Manager'.

'Go look for her lah.'

Yang finally met his old buddy's gaze. Ah Pui immediately held up his hand. 'Uh-uh-uh, don't give me the mushy thank you nonsense, okay? Just do what I say—go look for her, get married, and name your kid Ah Pui. Oh, and order the most expensive thing on the menu now. Your treat!'

Two evenings later, with her name card in hand, Yang made his way to Seah Street. Although a well-known food district, it was an area he seldom visited, its proximity to his home notwithstanding. His work had soaked up most of his time and energy all these years; when he was not at the fire station, he was either at home or visiting his Ma and Dai Kah Jie. Meals were simple, quick affairs at coffee shops nearby. The Central Fire Station had, in fact, been where his days and nights were mostly spent.

His footsteps slowed as he scanned, from a distance, the names of the eateries displayed on their shop fronts. Not the first one, nor the second, nor the third. He walked further into the lane. The place was abuzz with locals and tourists chatting over their meals in the row of restaurants, with some of the tables outside, alfresco style.

Finally, towards the end of the row, the words 'Nenek's Indonesian Kitchen' came into view. He stood at a distance, his heart beating much too quickly. Its décor warm and cozy, the restaurant was crowded, with the tables mostly filled. Light chatter interspersed with laughter greeted his ears.

He took a few steps forward; craned his neck to peer inside. A gentleman roughly his age was giving instructions to a staff as he attended to a customer. There was no sign of her.

He stood there for a few minutes. A waiter from the adjacent eatery approached him, asking if he would like a table.

The awkwardness of standing there, coupled with the uncertainty as to whether he was ready to meet her again, made his underarms wet with perspiration. He recalled her effervescence, and his reticence, whenever they visited street stalls in the past. What would he say to her if she now appeared before him, other than '*Hello, how have you been?*' Was that gentleman her boyfriend? Ah Pui had said she was not married, but that didn't mean she didn't have a boyfriend. What would he say to her, to him, to them?

Perhaps it would be best to come again another time, when the place was not so crowded.

A lady walked out from what must have been the kitchen of the restaurant. Full of smiles, she was carrying a tray of food, which she placed on one of the tables to appreciative nods from the diners there. She then walked over to the gentleman, who moved closer to her as he said something in her ear above the din of the crowd. Her familiar, warm attractiveness drew glances from patrons seated in the restaurant.

He took several steps back; drew in air with short, quick breaths. Three decades old, and still helpless against his own runaway, drumroll heartbeat.

With edgy steps, he hastened out of the lane, bumping into several people along the way.

'What? You went all the way there, then just walked away?' Ah Pui asked incredulously over the phone the next day, when he called Yang to find out how things went.

'It was crowded,' Yang replied defensively.

'So? You could have just gone in to say hello, right?'

'She was busy, okay? And—'

'And what?'

The line went silent.

'Eh, hello? Yang, are you still there? And what?'

'There was a guy with her.'

'Ohh. Now I understand. So, you chickened out. Competition, eh?'

'What do you know? You don't have a girlfriend.'

'Right, I don't. But I tell you what I know, okay? She's been trying to look for you. Why would she look for you if she has forgotten about you?'

'I don't know. To meet an old friend maybe.'

'You know what I think? That guy's her cousin. Wanna bet?'

Again, silence. Ah Pui went on, 'And you know what else I think? You're a chicken. You're brave enough to dash into a fire, but not brave enough to walk into her restaurant.'

Heavy, angry breaths rolled into Ah Pui's ears.

'I'll go again, okay? I didn't say I won't. And stop calling me a chicken, you fatty *kay-poh*. What's it got to do with you anyway?'

'Wah, angry ah! Fine. Call me whatever. She asked me to convey the message to you so that's what I'm doing.'

Silence.

Ah Pui sighed. 'Okay, I get it. You weren't prepared yesterday. After so long, I know, I know.'

'I didn't buy anything. And I didn't know what to say—'

'Can't you find an excuse to go? Let me think ah … like Valentine's Day?'

'Pui, it's April.'

'Okay, okay. Wait. Birthday?'

Ah Pui had hit on something. Her birthday was just a week away. She would be 26 this year.

'See? I got a good idea, right?' Ah Pui smirked when there was no reply, smacking his thigh. 'Her birthday's coming up, isn't it? Tell you what. Buy her a cake. And remember she likes mangoes? Buy some mangoes for her lah!'

'Mm.'

'And this time, go later at night? Then, when it's dark and romantic, pretend that your hand accidentally touches her hand, then—'

'Bye Pui.'

The phone line went dead on Ah Pui, who shrugged at the undemonstrative nature of his friend. He had become accustomed to it.

Five minutes later, the phone rang again. It was Ah Pui again.

'What is it again, Pui?'

'You need a haircut.'

'Huh?'

'Your hair was awful when I saw you. You sure you want to meet her like that?'

No answer.

Ah Pui persevered. 'I need to cut my hair too. Tomorrow, 7 o'clock. Usual place. Muthu Barber.'

This time the line went dead on Yang. Ah Pui had hung up without waiting for an answer.

The next day, Ah Pui was waiting outside 'Muthu Barber', where they had been getting their haircuts for years, when Yang arrived. The demonstrative Muthu waved a merry 'hello!' as they entered, smiling broadly as he pointed to two chairs.

'Haircut, boss?' Muthu asked.

'Yup,' Ah Pui replied, an impish look about him, his smile gleeful and sly, all at once. He winked at Muthu. 'Remember what I told you yesterday?'

'Ahh, yes, yes!' Muthu nodded profusely, returning the wink.

Yang turned towards Ah Pui, eyeing him suspiciously. 'What are you up to?'

'Nothing, nothing!' Ah Pui feigned innocence.

Muthu hunkered down to work, scissors in hand, snipping away dexterously. After half an hour, he slapped his hands in satisfaction.

'Ahh. There! Square fringe, layered, with a touch of the bowl. Vereee nice!'

Minutes later, lo and behold, two Bruce Lee lookalikes walked out of Muthu Barber. One fit, and one fat. One miffed, and one blithe.

The next morning, a team of firefighters in the Central Fire Station had a merry time with their new celebrity colleague. 'Bruce Lee Sir!' they greeted him in cheerful banter.

Chapter 27

Snow fiddled with the cassette player. Pressing the 'Play' button, she lay on the bed, listening to the sounds of the river, the squeaks of the otters. Her cousin had asked her to take the day off, today being her birthday, but she did not know where to go, nor what to do.

Why hadn't he come to look for her? Had Ah Pui passed him her name card? Ah Pui, in his typical blunt manner, had asked if she was married, to which she had grinned and said 'No'. Ah Pui had then happily offered the information that Yang was not married either. Not even a girlfriend, Ah Pui had said, sighing and shaking his head melodramatically, with a glint in his eye.

Unlike him, she had a boyfriend in Bandung. They had dated for a year, till he ended their relationship abruptly, finding excuses not to see her anymore, not to take her calls. She confronted him, and he admitted to having met someone else. That left a deep incision in her heart which took months to heal.

When her family set up a restaurant in Singapore, she had at first resisted coming back, had resisted leaving her Ma and Nenek, despite a strange desire to find out if he was doing well, if their friendship still meant anything to him, if … if what? She did not even know what it was that she wanted to find out.

Go. Go back. Look for him, Ma had said, the tip of her smile laced with a little sadness; a joyful ache perhaps shared by the mothers of this earth, when they gently nudge their little ones and then watch them soar into the sky; off and away, farther and farther, till they disappear.

You must search for your own life, Xue'er, Ma had gone on to say. Was that what she had come back to do? Yet, how did you search for something if you did not even know what it was? She asked herself if she still had affection for him; but perhaps she was asking all the wrong questions. Nine long years had passed. Surely, you could not simply shove love into the freezer as if it were a chicken and leave it there for years, and expect it to remain a chicken when you pull it out.

Perhaps all she could say was that he still held a special place in her heart, that what they had shared, had gone through together, was like a little stream in the river of her life, one which, though now obscured by the growth of new tributaries, would nevertheless always be a part of her. And, she had to admit, her heart had gone off in a tizzy when she saw him at the hotel collapse.

At 9 p.m., she left the apartment; walked listlessly along the streets, not knowing where she was heading. She soon found herself making the usual turn into Seah Street. The crowd was starting to thin out, with many of the eateries having just a table or two filled.

Reaching the end of the lane, she stopped. A man stood there, his back towards her; he held two paper bags and was staring into her restaurant. A familiar figure. Her pulse quickened. She stood there, certain and uncertain, all at once.

He continued to gaze through the glass entrance for a while. Slowly, he turned to leave, his eyes downcast. He took a step forward, then looked up.

Their eyes met. He gazed at her, his eyes conveying astonishment at her sudden appearance from behind him. Then a sort of suppressed joy seemed to come through as he began breathing more heavily. For a moment, she thought she saw a look of affection, but he quickly averted his gaze and gave an embarrassed cough. He cleared his throat as he looked at her again, a polite smile now on his face.

They stood there, the awkwardness of a nine-year separation occupying the less than nine feet of space between them. He saw that her eyes were as sincere and searching as they had been years ago. Her hair was cropped in the modern manner of a young, attractive professional.

He took a few steps towards her.

'I, er ... I ... you ...' he stuttered hopelessly, almost wishing he could kick himself for speaking like an idiot. He took a deep breath. 'I heard you're back. Ah Pui gave me your card.'

She nodded. 'I saw you. At the Hotel New World collapse.'

He remembered what he had brought and held these out to her.

'Happy birthday.'

An amused smile broke out on her face when she saw the mangoes in the bag. Her smile remained as infectious as ever.

'Thank you. How about taking a walk?' she asked.

He nodded.

They strolled to the Marina Bay. The esplanade was not crowded, but there were groups of people around—tourists taking photos, joggers having a night jog, couples holding hands. A light breeze drifted in from the sea.

He asked after her mother and Nenek and was glad to
know that they were well. He wanted to ask her why she had
come back; who the man in the restaurant was; how soon
she would be going back to Bandung. There were so many
questions he wanted to ask her, but did not know how best to
put them across.

'Salju Hartanto's your Indonesian name?' he asked, turning
to look at her as they walked along.

She nodded. 'Salju means snow. You know how we must
have more Indonesian-sounding names over there.'

'How's Bandung? You like it there?'

'Yeah. People there are warm and friendly. Nenek's family
is very big. They are good to us. They own a few restaurants in
Indonesia.'

They sat down on a bench facing the sea.

'And you? You joined the fire service?'

'Ya. People sometimes ask why. I myself don't know why.'

He gazed outward into the darkness of the water, and
inward into the darkness of his youth. Into the dark truth of his
Ma's words. Into the dark heart of the man she had parted with
on that last night.

'My Ma says that my whole life, I'm always fighting. Fighting
people. Fighting fires.'

She turned to look at him. His elbows were resting on his
knees, and his Bruce Lee haircut brought a tickled smile onto
her face.

'Your Ma should have named you Bruce,' she teased. 'Bruce
Lee, pirated version. Likes to fight.'

He turned to look at her. There was a cheeky grin on her
face and a twinkle in her eyes. She was still the spirited Snow he
had known. He smiled awkwardly.

'It was Ah Pui's silly idea,' he brought his hand to his hair, a
blush on his cheek.

'Sounds just like him,' she chuckled. 'It's cool. I like it.' Her tone became more serious. 'You saved many lives. It was so dangerous, tunnelling like that in the rubble. I ...' she paused, looking out at the ships in the distance, 'I was worried.'

He sighed. 'You know, I still see the dead bodies, still hear the cries for help. Sometimes, I wake up in cold sweat.' He fell silent for a minute. 'My job is unpredictable. Always on standby. Disaster can happen any time.'

'Do you feel scared when you are called to a fire?'

'Yeah. Me, my men, we do feel afraid. Once there was a child trapped in a fire. I had to go in. I was running out with the child when a beam fell on us. Luckily, my friend Alif came in to help us. Otherwise, I might not have made it.'

She listened intently without a word, the image of him carrying the child out of a raging fire before her eyes. She then thought of her mother, trapped in the fire long ago. Maybe, if the firefighters could have reached her, her face would not have been burned. She would not have been disfigured. Would not be blind.

'Ah Pui told me you came back to run your family's restaurant,' he continued.

'Mm-hmm. I came back with my cousin. Maybe you saw him at the restaurant.'

'I see. So, he's your cousin.'

'Yeah. Who did you think he was?'

'Oh, I don't know ... I mean, I didn't think anything ...' he fumbled with his words, turning red again. Best to change the subject. 'How long will you be here?'

'I don't know. Maybe a few months, maybe a few years.'

She fiddled with the carrier bag on her lap, the one with the birthday cake he had bought for her, as the question which had tossed about in her mind for years came to the fore.

'Yang, I've been wanting to ask you something. For a long time, ever since I left, I've been wondering … about you selling cassettes, and, getting into trouble because of that … was it because of me? To help me at the shop?'

He looked up suddenly, not expecting such a question. It took a while before he said something.

'I was selling pirated cassettes since I was a kid. Getting into fights since my childhood. When I helped in your shop, I couldn't work at the coffee shop. And I needed to support my Ma, help Dai Kah Jie. So …' he stopped.

A couple, holding hands, walked past them. For a time, neither of them spoke.

Finally, he said, 'It's getting late. I'll see you home.'

As they stood up to leave, she turned to face him. 'I want to invite you and your family to my restaurant, for dinner. To thank you for helping my family back then. I didn't even have a chance to thank you properly.'

He nodded, then looked at her for a moment, his eyes searching as he met her gaze, captivated once more by the authenticity in her eyes.

Chapter 28

One evening two weeks later, Yang took his Ma, Dai Kah Jie, and Yee Kah Jie to Snow's restaurant.

Her cousin Budi warmly welcomed them. His smile was genuine as he said to Yang, 'My grandaunt, Salju's Nenek, tells us how much you helped our family. So happy to meet you. Salju's in the kitchen. She'll be out shortly.'

Ah Pui and Snow's friend, Meiyun, were already seated at a table. Snow had invited them as well, and Ah Pui was happily helping himself to the basket of *keropok*, or crackers, on the table. He stood up to greet them. 'Ah-Yee! Kah Jies! Long time no see!' He offered the *keropok* to the ladies, after which he held one out to Yang. 'Here she comes!' he whispered, nudging his friend.

Snow came out from the kitchen. A smile lent a warm glow to her face when she saw them. She greeted Yang's mother and sisters genially, noticing the small scar on his mother's face but ensuring that her gaze did not linger. Dai Kah Jie and Yee Kah Jie gave sincere smiles; Ma a polite one.

'Yang helped me and my family many years ago. I've not been able to thank him, and you, properly, till now,' she said to them. Ma nodded, then turned away so that her scar would not be conspicuous.

Dinner was served. Snow was busy going in and out of the kitchen, managing to catch just a few minutes with them from time to time. Dai Kah Jie and Yee Kah Jie had a good time reminiscing with Ah Pui about the good old days. Ma sat there stiffly, eating but not speaking much, keeping the scarred side of her face turned away as much as possible.

A young gentleman seated alone at a nearby table watched Snow as she went to and from the kitchen. He seemed acquainted with Snow; they exchanged brief conversations when she brought food to his table. Yang observed wryly that the man had a peculiar mop of hair, with spiky, gelled tufts sprouting like the head of a pineapple.

He recognized the look in Mr. Pineapple-head's eyes; he knew what it meant when a man looked at a woman thus, and he stiffened in his seat. The burn in his chest took him somewhat by surprise.

'Bothered, bro?' Ah Pui teased, glancing in Pineapple-head's direction, then lowering his voice, 'Meiyun says that guy's been coming here every day.'

'That Pineapple-head guy?' Yang scoffed.

'Pineapple-head, ha!' Ah Pui guffawed, slapping his friend's shoulder. 'He sure burns you like a pineapple, man! Don't say I didn't warn you. You better work fast. She's attractive.'

Snow walked towards their table with a platter of fruits, but Pineapple-head intercepted her, seemingly asking her about something on the menu. Yang stood up; walked over. He placed his hand lightly on her elbow, smiled an 'Excuse us' to Pineapple-head, and walked her over to their table.

She placed the fruit platter on the table and joined them. Ah Pui began chuckling. On the plate were three kinds of sliced fruit—mango on the left, papaya on the right, and lots of pineapple in between.

'What so funny?' Snow asked Ah Pui.

'Oh, nothing, nothing!' He gave a wicked grin as he lifted the fruit platter and began sliding the pineapple slices onto Yang's plate.

'I didn't know you liked pineapple,' Snow remarked to Yang.

'I don't,' Yang replied, chomping on the pineapple, wincing from the burn on his tongue.

'Ya, he doesn't like pineapple. He likes mango!' Ah Pui chimed in.

'So, he likes mango, and he doesn't like pineapple. But you're making him eat all the pineapple on the plate?' Snow quizzed Ah Pui, brow raised in curiosity.

'Bingo!' Ah Pui slid the last slice of pineapple onto Yang's plate. 'Ta da!' He placed the fruit platter back on the table, with its mango on one side, papaya on the other, and no more pineapple in between.

After dinner, Snow walked with Ah Pui and Yang's family onto the street. Her cousin Budi walked with Yang behind them.

Budi said in a hushed tone to Yang, 'Nenek asked me to tell you something. She says that Salju came back to look for you.'

Yang turned to look at Budi, his eyes questioning, somewhat taken aback by what Budi had just revealed. He then turned to look at the back of Snow's figure as she chatted with Dai Kah Jie. His heart seemed to pull in opposing directions. He did not like the attention she received from other men. If it was true that he had been fighting his whole life, he now wanted to fight for her, fight to be with her, fight to love her. Yet, perhaps, his Ma was right. Which girl would want to marry a man with such a dangerous job? And even if she had feelings for him, did he want her to live a life of worry? Before, he had felt inadequate in his ability to provide for and protect her. Now, even as he had attained this ability, being with him would itself give rise to uncertainty and anxiety.

Budi walked ahead to bid farewell to Yang's family. Snow turned back, walked towards Yang.

'I'll call you later,' he said gently to her.

She saw in his eyes the same tenderness she had seen years ago. She looked at him, the nervous recognition of his affection blushing onto her face as she nodded.

Chapter 29

The fire alarm at the Central Fire Station rang. Yang, Alif, and their team slid down the pole to the fire engine bay. Within minutes they were racing towards a reported fire at a shop along Beach Road.

The large blaze had engulfed two adjacent shops on the ground floor of the block and was spreading fast. Billows of thick smoke choked the air. The firefighters aimed their water jets at the menacing tongues of fire as they tried to ascertain if anyone was trapped inside.

'Alif! Evacuate everyone!' Yang shouted above the roar of the inferno and the screams of fleeing people. The overpowering waves of burning heat throbbed forcefully into them, like the raging heart of a violent beast ready to devour the ten firefighters battling it.

Yang directed the jet of water towards the heart of the fire. He edged forward in the same way he had advanced towards the many fires he had had to contend with over the years— cautiously assessing the enemy's trajectory, pushing against the heat, becoming conscious of the rising, burning force in his own heart which propelled him forward, a force that could perhaps only be described as madness, a malady of the unseen self; a compulsion to confront a visible opponent with an invisible flame of inadequacy; of fearing yet wanting to fight, of needing to fight to prove that he did have what it took to put up a fight.

He moved closer to the flames. Then, without warning, an incandescent light engulfed his consciousness. There was a sudden sound, like the crack of a whip, silencing all other sounds. It was as if he had been thrust abruptly into an unknown dimension in that single moment, his being floating in a soundless, timeless space, where the only sounds were voices from his memory.

He opened his eyes but could not tell where he was, lying, as it were, on his back and looking at the blue, cloudless sky above. He pushed himself up with his elbow and palm. With a heave both resolute and unsteady, he stood up.

The 8 p.m. news on the radio broadcast came on. The restaurant often tuned in to the radio station; the music played on air accompanied the patrons along with their meals. The radio deejay mentioned a large fire along Beach Road earlier that day. An explosion had occurred which had injured several firefighters and shop owners.

Snow stopped in her tracks, the tray of piping hot food in her hands, the voice of the radio deejay drifting into syllables her mind was no longer processing. Yang was supposed to be on duty at the fire station today.

Budi walked over. He asked if she wanted to look Yang up to make sure he was all right. She nodded as she cast a grateful glance at her cousin, who had been like an elder brother to her.

She stepped out into the night, her heartbeat quickening as she walked briskly to the main road, where she raised her hand to flag down a taxi, but it was difficult to hail a taxi at this hour in this part of the town. It was twenty minutes before she did manage to climb into one. In the ten minutes it took to reach the Central Fire Station, she found her palms moist with cold perspiration, her untamed thoughts heading in all directions.

Climbing out of the taxi, she looked at the fire station. It was quiet outside the red-bricked building, with no one around, and she could not enter. In her frantic rush to get here, she had not considered this. She paced outside the station, hoping to meet one of the firefighters who came out.

On the road the cars sped by. Across the road, the Funan Mall continued to unleash people from its confines, prodding them towards the safety of their own homes with the deepening of the night. The fire station stood impassive, unstirred by the flurry of vehicles and people around it. No one entered, and no one came out.

Unruly fears weighed her down. It was now close to 10 p.m. She got into another taxi. To Cantonment Road, she told the driver.

Twenty minutes later, she knocked on the door, checking to make sure she was knocking on the correct door; he had given her his address, but she had not been to his place as yet.

No answer. She knocked again.

'Yang, are you there? It's me, Snow,' she called out.

Finally, the door opened. He stood there in a T-shirt and shorts, surprised to see her at the door. There was a bandage around his neck.

'Oh,' he said. 'Come in. Sorry, I took so long. Had to pull on a T-shirt, and took a while, with the bandage and all.'

She stepped inside, her eyes still on the bandage. 'I heard on the radio. About the fire,' she said almost breathlessly. 'The explosion.'

He looked at her slightly ruffled hair, her anxious eyes.

'Yeah. I ...' he searched for the words to say to her, to tell her what had happened, but could not find them; how was he to tell her that in that moment he had flown through the air, he had heard her voice, and had been terrified that he might not see her again?

'I'm okay. My suit protected me. Just some burns on my neck. Minor, not serious,' he said softly.

She gazed up at him with pulsating emotions which she could no longer hold captive inside.

'I ... I was so worried,' she whispered, her voice choking up.

He gazed at her, at the agony in her eyes, at the tension in her body, all of which penetrated deep into his heart, hurling an accusatory voice at him, telling him that he was the cause of her pain, that his fears had come true, that he would be the one to hurt her after all, the same way he had hurt her so many years ago.

'Sorry ...' was all he could utter, his chest tightening.

He placed his hand gently on her cheek. She took hold of his hand, clasping it to her face. A tremendous swell of tenderness was pushing through him—a tenderness which spurred a powerful swathe of desire as much as it inhibited its synchronous surge—the force of which he now succumbed to, compelling him to draw deep, heavy breaths as he held her face in both his hands, looked deep into her eyes. She saw the affection he had felt for her all these aching years finally flowing through, affection which he had worked so hard to hold back for so long, now set free in his eyes. He kissed her forehead—

how long had it been since he had longed to kiss her, to hold her in his arms?

He placed his arm around her waist, pulled her gently towards him. Bringing his face close, he tenderly placed his lips against hers, as she put her arms around him and felt the warmth of his breath, of his face, of his body.

They talked late into the night, sitting side by side on the floor, leaning against the sofa, her arm looped around his, his hand holding hers.

He opened up to her about his family, about how his father had left them; about his mother blaming him for his father's abandonment; about Dai Kah Jie slogging at the wet market to support the family; about Long Kor being like a brother to him, with whom he sold pirated cassettes and got into fights, but who ensured he did not get involved in other, more serious criminal activities.

She talked about the relationship she had in Bandung and its abrupt end which left her deeply hurt; about her life in Bandung in those initial years when she missed him so; about her growing years in Singapore during which her parents struggled with her mother's blindness and facial disfigurement.

'Why didn't you tell me you were selling cassettes because of me? That you couldn't come to the provision shop cos you feared for my safety?' she asked him at one point.

After a long pause, he said, 'I didn't know how to tell you, about my past. With the gangs.' He then turned to face her— he had to turn his entire body, for the bandage on his neck rendered it impossible to turn his head—and held her shoulders as he said, 'I made up my mind to put all that behind. After that last night at the river.'

She nodded. 'Do you know, when I saw you come out of the tunnel, at the hotel collapse, I was so happy to have found you, but also so worried?' She then placed her hand on his arm, smiling slightly as she continued, 'And, I was so proud of you.'

He embraced her, stroked her hair, telling her that the Kallang River had been transformed, that the farms had been cleared, the kampong dwellers moved to HDB flats, and the hawkers relocated to food centres around the island. It was now clean but manicured—neat, prim and proper, unlike its original character.

She soon dozed off, her head leaning against his shoulder. He helped her up, gave her one of his T-shirts to change into, tucked her into his bed, and pulled the blanket snugly over her. He then took a spare pillow to sleep on the sofa.

As he turned to leave the bedroom, he beheld her figure lying on his bed. A deep sense of peace blanketed him, as if a glorious fall of rain sent by the heavens had brought new life to the dry, parched land of his existence.

She woke up to the aroma of scrambled eggs wafting out of the kitchen. He was standing at the stove, sprinkling a generous amount of salt on the eggs in the frying pan.

'The sun's out and it's raining salt in here?' she teased, standing behind him and peeking over his shoulder.

He turned around, and she came face to face with a large, bright sun printed on his apron. Her hand was now over her mouth, trying to suppress a peal of laughter.

'What's so funny?' he asked in earnest.

'Nothing, Mr. Sun,' she chuckled. 'Now my turn to scramble eggs, and we see whose tastes better?'

He grinned. 'Okay, why not?'

As she stood in front of the stove, he wrapped his arms around her waist from behind, his cheek touching hers, his apron-sun kissing her back.

'Your neck's going to hurt,' she teased, and he smiled.

Chapter 30

Their wedding was to take place on 1 September 1987. It was to be a simple affair—solemnization at the Registry of Marriages followed by dinner for family and close friends at a restaurant at nearby Fort Canning. A dinner celebration would be held in Bandung a week later for relatives and friends in Bandung.

Snow's family flew in from Bandung a week before the wedding. The two families met for the first time at the Red Star Chinese restaurant along Chin Swee Road. Yang, his Ma, and two sisters waited at a table. He had told his Ma that Snow's family once lived in Kampong Bukit Ho Swee as well but did not mention that Ba had once delivered Pepsi bottles to their provision shop, for he and his sisters had long learnt not to bring up the past with Ma.

When Snow arrived with her family—her Ma, Nenek, Budi and his father—heads turned along with the rise of hushed murmurings at surrounding tables. People gawked at the blind woman with the disfigured face. Snow, her Ma, and their family walked on stoically, heads held high, holding out against the worldly hostility which had accompanied their lives all these years.

Yang's mother gaped at her soon-to-be in-law. She shifted her stare to the sprightly old woman, recognizing her as Nenek, the woman who owned a provision shop in the kampong. Nenek approached the table with her blind daughter-in-law, nephew, and grandnephew, smiling broadly, warmly, as she extended her greetings. Snow's Ma nodded, smiling kindly at those whom she could not see, who would soon be family.

Having greeted them, Yang turned towards his Ma, who appeared shaken as they took their seats. He wondered if he should have better prepared her, should have told her about the facial disfigurement, the blindness. He glanced at Snow, who smiled wistfully as she took in his mother's reaction. He reached for her hand below the table, held it tightly, as her Nenek broke the ice in her characteristic genial manner.

That night, in the quiet of her room, Yang's mother sat stiffly at the edge of her bed. After a while, she stood up and walked over to a corner of her room. She placed her hand on the sheet of cloth draping her sewing machine. Gently, carefully, she pulled the cloth away.

She ran her hands slowly along the contours of the precious object—along the metal wheel, along the wooden spine, along the intricate metal structures along which the threads would run. Her hand moved along tenderly, lovingly, longingly, on the prized possession bought by a husband for his wife. Her hand came to rest on the scar on her face.

She had to go back. Once again, she saw the flames, breathed in the smoke, heard the screams. She felt her heart racing as she ran back into the attap house, pushed the heavy sewing machine out with all her might. She saw the panic of those carrying their possessions, running away, like her. She was running and pushing. Running and pushing. And then she had to stop.

Now, standing in her bedroom twenty-six years later, her heart was beating as rapidly as it did on that fateful day. Abruptly, she snapped out of her involuntary recollection. No, she told herself. She did not remember any more. She did not want to remember any more. The fire was not her fault. She was a victim, wasn't she? She had always been a pitiful person in this life; life which had dealt her a poor hand time and again, hadn't she?

She placed the cloth back over the sewing machine. Life had never been kind to her, she repeated to herself. The past should remain covered beneath the cloth she had preserved her entire married, and later no-longer-married, life. Secrets should remain hidden from the world, safely tucked away, shrouded in the dark.

Chapter 31

The first shafts of light welcomed the new day—the day of the wedding—as they did the new month of September.

Snow sat in front of the mirror at the dressing table in her room, her Nenek fussing over the position of her tiara. Her mother walked in.

'*Boleh*! *Chantek*! My lovely granddaughter,' Nenek exclaimed, holding Snow's shoulders, both of them beaming into the mirror.

Nenek turned towards Snow's mother. '*Chantek, kita anak.*' she told her daughter-in-law how beautiful their child was. Ma nodded, a smile on her face.

Ma held her daughter's hand. She gently ran her hand along the exquisite fabric and lace of the wedding gown, along the intricate tiara pinned to her daughter's hair, along the veil—now pushed back—which would later hold the resplendence of the bride's face in its bosom, along the contours of the soft, warm face she had never stopped longing to see.

She placed her hand on her daughter's cheek. In the silence of her heart, she blessed her daughter, sending an unuttered prayer to the heavens for a loving marriage, for a happy, peaceful life with a man who would take care of her.

Snow brought her hand to her mother's face. She wiped away the tear that had rolled down her mother's cheek. Her mother smiled from the depths of her warm, lonely heart as they sat, hands clasped in one another's.

At the Registry of Marriages, they took their vows. He held his wife's hand tenderly as he placed the wedding band on her finger, as she did with his. He lifted the veil. They kissed to the applause of their families, to the cheers of the best man, Ah Pui, and the bridesmaid, Meiyun.

That night, in the dim lighting of their bedroom, she beheld all the scars on his body—the one on his neck from the fire explosion; the one on his elbow where a deep gash had opened his flesh as he dug and crawled in the earth in search of survivors; the one on his thigh where the beam had fallen when he dashed into the fire to save the child; the one on his arm where he had been cut long ago from fighting with other men.

Tenderly, she ran her hand along the contours of his body, along the contours of his scars. He kissed her forehead as she lay in his arms. He pulled her closer, brought his lips to hers, ran his hands down the contours of her body.

In that moment, there was no need to fight any more.

Outside, a light fall of rain blessed the earth, even as the moon smiled upon the petunias and the peacock flowers, a smile reflected in the mirrors of the glass droplets on the leaves, and in the scent of the rain and the earth lifted up in the broad arms of the bird's nest ferns. The rain reminded the flowers, the shrubs, and the trees of their renewed lushness, as their roots took in the coolness of the water, and their leaves bathed in the radiance of the moonlight.

Deep in the soil lay the body of a rotting centipede. A poisonous secret, buried and hidden, deep below the world. Amid the rain that had seeped into the darkness of the land, it had already begun its pungent journey of release and reconciliation with the earth.

Part Four

Air

Light and life gifted by the sun
Yet scars are overflowing
Washing the parched land
Into brave, lonely seas
Earth, poisoned abundance
Cries out in song
The air beckons
Courage's scent rises

***

1994

Chapter 32

Yang woke up to the wind-blown rain pattering on the windowpanes as the dawn began her painting of orange hues beyond the dark clouds in the sky. With eyes half opened, he got out of bed; walked with haphazard step to the window, and pulled it shut.

Snow lay asleep. Fatigue had defined her days of late, in the same way it had three years ago, when they had awaited their first child, only to lose the child in a miscarriage. Now, she was with child once again. It was early stages yet, and the doctor had advised as much bed rest as was possible. She had not been to her restaurant for two weeks now.

It being a Saturday notwithstanding, he had to be back in the office for a meeting. Rising through the ranks over the years, he was now a deputy director at the Singapore Civil Defence Force (SCDF), which had merged with the Singapore Fire Service after the Hotel New World collapse. He had worked hard, had undergone training overseas, in the UK and Japan. They had bought a HDB flat in Kallang, where they now lived.

She opened her eyes a little; saw him sitting on the bed. 'Going to work so early?' she asked wearily.

He reached out to caress her hair. 'Hmm. I'll cook some eggs and leave it on the table for you, okay?'

'No need. I can cook myself,' she muttered, closing her eyes.

Later that morning, she found a plate of scrambled eggs on the dining table. Beside it was a bunch of keys—his house keys. He had forgotten his keys, again, and she would have to remain at home, remain awake, till he got home. She looked from the eggs to the keys and did not know whether to smile or to sigh.

A week later, she was back at the restaurant, glad to be back at work again. Yang had not been entirely convinced that she should resume work, though he knew that she had been away from the restaurant for almost a month, and that it was difficult lying in bed all day long, when Budi was barely able to cope.

The aromatic flavours of *Ayam Bakar*—Indonesian grilled chicken—wafted in the air, making her stomach churn. She held her breath, soldiering on with the usual frenzy that came with the dinner crowd. The restaurant had grown in both reputation and size, having expanded to include the adjacent unit. Budi had hired more staff, but they were still swamped with orders this time of day.

In the kitchen, she sat down for a moment, breathless and flushed. It had been similar three years ago, when she was expecting their first child. She—they—had lost that child. Now, she placed her hand gently on her abdomen, on the child inside. She went to the telephone, paged for Yang, asked if he could come by to the restaurant, to accompany her home.

She heard his silent hesitation over the phone. A fire had broken out in which one of his men had been injured, he said, and he had to submit an incident report. He could come by if she could wait for him. She told him that she would make her own way home.

He was often busy with his work, as she had been with hers, and, as with any marriage, they had their ups and downs over the years, but by and large, he had been a good husband, treating her with kindness and respect.

She was panting by the time she reached home, her brow creased with vexation at being breathless from a task as basic as walking up two flights of stairs. She staggered into their bedroom and lay down on the bed.

He got home an hour later; came to sit beside her, placing his palm on her pale cheek.

'Are you okay?'

She nodded. His pager beeped.

'Is it your office?' she asked.

'No. It's Ma.' He walked out to telephone his mother, then came back in. 'Ma wants me to go over. She says she had a fall.'

'You better go. I'm okay. Just need to rest,' she said feebly, so tired that she could barely keep her eyes open. He pulled the blanket over her. 'I'll be back as soon as I can,' he said before he left.

She did not know how long she slept. It could have been ten minutes, or it could have been two hours. But she was awakened by a pain in her abdomen that was as familiar as it was foreboding.

She looked around for him, called out for him. He was not back. Frantically, she reached for the telephone and paged for him.

Chapter 33

She opened her eyes, looked around at the nurses going about their duties, at the other patients lying on the beds beside hers. The smell of antiseptic and the sight of Yang talking to a doctor at the nurses' station, his expression downcast, filtered through the clouds of consciousness.

Gradually, the fear she had felt came back. The distraught call for a taxi. The ride which she could not remember, save for the panic. The kind taxi driver who helped her out of the vehicle. The subsequent ride lying on the wheeled trolley, all alone.

Gradually, the pain, or rather its twin—its memory, its shadow—came back. The struggle down the stairs, down the lift. The cramp in her abdomen. The helplessness when, upon reaching the hospital, the nurses asked if she was alone, if her husband was on his way. The same anguish she had felt three years ago when she lost their child; again, a twin, this time real, not a memory, not a shadow.

Why did pain seem to have a knack for replicating itself?

And a dark wave of sadness, so cold it numbed her, washed over her entire being.

He came over; sat down on the chair beside her bed. After some time, he placed his hand on hers. 'Sorry' was all he said.

She did not move; did not look at him. Was his Ma okay after her fall, she asked, her gaze still averted. He said yes, she was fine. He had informed her Ma and Nenek, he continued, and they would fly in from Bandung soon.

'Thank you,' she said softly, her eyes still unable to meet his. Then, after a long silence, all she could utter was that same word—sorry.

Perhaps, she just wanted—needed—to be alone. Perhaps there was anger. Or guilt. Or fear that he would blame her. Or grief that would overpower her if she looked at him. She did not know, for nothing made any sense at this moment.

He sat there silently beside her, as she drifted in and out of sleep. When she opened her eyes later, the chair was empty.

He walked the streets alone for a long time, that night.

By the time he arrived at the hospital, it was too late. Too late to see her. Too late to hold her hand, to comfort her. Too late to save their child. Too late to say goodbye.

Yet—and here, a sudden surge of anger rose within him— hadn't he dissuaded her from going back to work? Wasn't she at fault as well, and hadn't he held his tongue at the hospital, refrained from saying, *I told you not to go back to work*?

She had not looked at him as she lay in the hospital. He could feel her anguish, but he could not reach her. What the chasm that separated them was made of, he did not know. Perhaps, there was anger on both sides. She had insisted on going back to work. He had not been there when she needed to get to the hospital quickly.

The line between life and death was often as thin, as elusive, as the breath of a minute. He had learnt this from years of encounters with those fiery tongues which wrangled and contended with him, with his men, ruthlessly taking a living person into their embrace in a matter of minutes.

They had had seven good years. Although her miscarriage three years ago had been difficult, they had been told that it was not uncommon, and they had continued to be hopeful. She had brought a deep sense of calm and peace into his life. It sounded trite, but he had felt contented, felt happy.

Now, as he listened to the exhalation of his own breath, it seemed to him that life, love, joy—all the good things of this world—were as fleeting as a breath of air.

Snow lay on the bed, staring at the ceiling. As someone touched her lightly on the arm, she turned around.

A grey-haired, elderly woman smiled kindly at her. Introducing herself as Madam Tan, she offered Snow a bowl of chicken soup. Her daughter, who had just undergone a hysterectomy, was asleep on the bed beside Snow. She had boiled a pot of the soup for her daughter, who could not drink all of it. Snow accepted the woman's kindness.

'How's your daughter?' Snow asked.

Madam Tan sighed, her eyes clouding over. 'She has ovarian cancer. She's only thirty-eight.'

Snow placed her hand gently on Madam Tan's arm. The elderly woman acknowledged with a sad smile, then returned to her daughter's bed. Snow glanced at the young woman, merely four years older than she was, lying on the adjacent bed, fighting a terminal illness. Her own loss was not the only pain in the world.

Perhaps, her coldness towards Yang had been too harsh. She had not meant it; did not understand why she could not even look at him. It was not his fault. She knew that. The sting of the realization had simply rendered her incapable of any emotional proximity with another, he being her husband and the father of her child notwithstanding. Perhaps, it was precisely because he was the father of the child she had failed to protect.

The familiar sound of her mother's walking stick grew louder. *Tap, tap, tap*—the rhythm of her mother's life, the embodiment of her loss, the sound of pushing on with an unfinished journey. At that moment, it was the sound of unspeakable comfort.

Ma and Nenek appeared at the doorway. The other patients and the visitors in the room turned to stare at Ma's face. Some gasped. That, too, was the sound of her mother's life. Right now, it did not bother her. The two women came to sit on the bed beside her, reached to hold her hand, and the convoluted agony finally flowed freely.

In the embrace of Ma and Nenek, the oppressive pull of grief lightened a little. Seeing them brought great solace, for she missed them dearly. After her marriage, she had returned to Bandung once or twice yearly, for a few weeks each time. She had not seen them for eight months.

Nenek's hair had grown whiter. Now seventy-nine years old, she was still strong and spritely. Nenek told her that Yang had gone to the airport to pick them up, had sent them to the hospital, telling them, hesitantly, that it might be better that he did not come with them. He did not want to make her feel worse, he had said.

Ma squeezed her hand. 'He's hurting too,' she said.

Snow pressed her hand into Ma's palm. 'I know, Ma.'

With some measure of calmness settling into her spent spirit, she found herself hoping that he would come to see her later. Ma was right. She should not have been so hostile towards him.

Madam Tan came over. Addressing Nenek, she asked affably, 'Nenek? From Kampong Bukit Ho Swee?'

The two elderly women looked at each other, smiles of recognition soon spreading across their faces. 'Ah Gek!' Nenek exclaimed.

The two women held on to the other's arm in the buoyant manner of old friends meeting again. Madam Tan was an old neighbour from the kampong. As with many of their neighbours, they had lost contact after the fire that changed their lives over thirty years ago.

Madam Tan, glancing at Ma, asked Nenek, 'This is Su Mei, your daughter-in-law? And how's your son?'

'Su Mei was caught in the fire,' Nenek explained, sighing. 'And my son, he had a heart attack. Eighteen years already.'

'Oh. I see,' Madam Tan sighed, placing a hand on Nenek's arm in a consoling gesture, with the other hand reaching to hold Ma's hand. Ma smiled warmly as she held the elderly woman's hand.

Later, Madam Tan offered to keep Snow company while Ma and Nenek went back to get some rest. Nenek gave a bunch of grapes to Snow and another to Madam Tan, who came to sit with Snow after Ma and Nenek left. She appeared to be pondering something, absorbed in her thoughts.

She asked Snow if her mother had told them how her burn injuries had been sustained during the fire. Snow related to Madam Tan that her mother remembered being hit by something from behind.

Madam Tan nodded pensively. 'Your mother was good-looking. And kind,' she said, with a distant look in her eyes. 'I saw her from a distance. During the fire. I didn't know ...' her voice trailed off.

She then looked at Snow with seriousness in her eyes.

'I saw what happened that day,' she said, her voice soft but resolute. 'I saw what had hit your mother from behind.'

Snow felt a jolt of surprise. Her breathing quickened; she clutched the grape she had been holding in her hand tightly.

'You saw?' she asked, unable to believe what she was hearing.

The older woman nodded slowly. 'I was not too far from your Ma. Everyone was running away. I was also running away, like your Ma.'

'Then?' Snow gasped, all formality now thrown aside.

'Then, I saw a woman, pushing a sewing machine. She had to stop because her path was blocked by a few people in front of her,' she paused, pulling back the memory. 'Your Ma was one of the people blocking her way.'

Madam Tan looked into the distance beyond the window, anger fanning the frown on her brows, sadness extending into her eyes. 'I saw her push the sewing machine towards your Ma and another neighbour, Cheong Soh. From the back.'

Snow looked down, bewildered. Was it a sewing machine that had hit her mother?

'After that, I lost sight of them. My husband pulled me along, shouting, "What are you looking at? Run!" So, I ran with him.'

'Did you see who the woman was? Do you know her?' Snow asked, her pulse racing.

'Yes,' she said. 'We all knew one another in the kampong.'

Snow waited for Madam Tan to carry on, her restlessness transmitted to the clutched grape in her hand.

The older woman finally broke her silence. 'It was Ah Feng. Her husband used to deliver Pepsi to your family's provision shop.'

A small, helpless grape suddenly hit the floor, falling from the clutches of a hand. It made nary a sound as its soft flesh struck the hard surface, rolling away in confusion, till it came to rest, baffled. Stunned.

Chapter 34

She placed her passport on the check-in counter, together with the passports of her Ma and Nenek.

'Heading to Bandung?' the lady in the Garuda Airlines uniform behind the counter asked, smiling at the passenger who had a somewhat listless air about her.

'Yes,' Snow replied indifferently.

She took the three boarding passes; strode to where Ma, Nenek, and Yang were waiting in the departure hall. Yang, leaning against a wall, glanced at her when she walked over, then shifted his gaze towards the floor.

Nenek looked from her granddaughter to her grandson-in-law, sighed, and shook her head in incomprehension. Ma reached out to hold her daughter's hand, saying, 'It's still early. Go talk to him. We wait here for you.'

She walked over to where he was standing. He looked up at his wife. She had lost weight, had grown thin. There was a tiredness in the way her hair was pushed behind her ears, with loose strands straggling down the side of her face. Her eyes held a shield of dullness behind which her pain was hidden. Her sadness sat like a sting in his heart, dissipating whatever anger there had been earlier. Yet, he could not comfort her. Upon her discharge from the hospital, she had requested to stay with her Ma and Nenek in Budi's apartment. When they were alone together, in moments like this when she stood beside him, she would not even look at him.

'Will you walk with me?' he asked softly.

She nodded, her gaze on the floor. He wanted to hold her hand, but she tucked both her hands into her pockets as they walked in silence towards the airport viewing gallery. The planes came into view beyond the glass facade.

He stopped walking, and she took his cue. He turned to face her.

'I'm sorry. For not being there. For what happened. Please talk to me,' he pleaded gently.

His words, his tenderness, his anguish—these burned into her heart, kindling the warmth and affection buried there, yet in the same stroke, scalding the bruised flesh. How she longed to talk to him; longed to bask in his tender gaze, to look at him, to place her hand in his, to tell him she did not blame him for the loss of their child, to rest in his arms again—if only he knew.

Yet, how did you gaze into the eyes of the man whose mother had ruined the life of your own mother? How was a wife to tell her husband that his mother had destroyed her family; that in the tempestuous heat of that long-ago fire lay a chilling secret that had lain hidden for over thirty years?

She turned to face him without meeting his gaze. 'Please give me some time,' she struggled to draw in her breaths. 'I need to be alone. I'm sorry.'

He saw the tears streaked on her face. He hesitated, then lifted his hand toward her face. Seeing his hand, her heart raced wildly, as if something terrifying had come between them, something that had come before him, but that continued to stretch its ugly hand towards her; and all seemed lost between the two of them now—their marriage, their child, their love, the years of companionship—for the thing that had come between them was nothing less than the ugly hand of truth.

And in that instant, almost involuntarily, she took a step back; drew away from his touch.

His hand remained in mid-air for a second, his breathing now heavy, an intense bewilderment fleeting across his eyes. He put his hand down; looked down, trying not to let the hurt, the despondency, convey themselves beyond his eyes.

He took deep breaths, steadied himself.

'How long … will you be away?'

'Maybe a few weeks. I'll let you know.'

They stood side by side, looking at the planes. One was moving at great speed along the runway, picking up even more energy before it lifted its nose towards the sky, bringing its wings up, bringing a hundred lives into the air, some towards reunion with those they loved, others towards separation from those they loved.

'It's time to board,' he said without looking at her.

They turned and made their way back to the departure hall.

Chapter 35

Bandung, Indonesia

Snow placed the *Martabak Manis*, the sweet pancake popular in Indonesia, on the dining table; she had gone for a walk and had passed by a shop selling the snack her Ma and Nenek loved.

Budi's parents—her uncle and his wife—and Nenek were watching TV in the living area. Ma was in the small garden of their old terrace house, where she often sat for hours.

Snow sat down on a rattan chair beside Ma; placed a warm packet of *Martabak Manis* in her hands. Ma smiled. They sat in quiet companionship for a while, taking in the cheerful laughter of the neighbours' children and the fragrance of *Nasi Padang* being prepared in the houses along their street, Jalan Sumber Mulya.

'Xue'er, what happened with you and Yang?' Ma asked. 'I know it's painful, the miscarriage. Sometimes, in life, there are things we can never get back. Like your child. Like my face. My sight.'

Ma reached out to hold Snow's hand. Snow relished her mother's touch, the warmth of which, along with the comfort of her mother's voice, had filled the spaces in her life rendered void by her mother's blindness and facial disfigurement.

'Ma, during the fire, long ago, in the kampong, were you running away with some of the neighbours?'

Ma nodded. 'I was running with our neighbour Cheong Soh. We both fell when something hit us from the back. Cheong Soh was burned on her arm. My hair caught fire. Some people later ran over to help us.'

'Have you ever thought about what could have hit you?'

Ma turned her head slightly towards Snow, surprised by the unexpected questions. She turned back to face the trees along the street, looking ahead with her unseeing eyes.

'At the beginning, I used to think. All the time. But after a while, what's the point?'

'Were you hit around your hips?'

'I think so.'

'So, maybe, it was a sewing machine?'

Ma turned towards Snow. 'Xue'er, why are you asking?'

Snow squeezed her mother's hands. 'Remember the old neighbour from the kampong, the lady we met at the hospital? She ...' she struggled to carry on. 'She told me, she said she saw ... saw what happened.'

Ma's hand gave a startled jerk, her muscles tensing. She said nothing but continued to listen intently.

'She said that she saw a woman pushing a sewing machine behind you. You and Cheong Soh were blocking her way. She ... pushed the sewing machine towards you. From behind,' Snow found that breathing was becoming an increasingly difficult task. 'Ma ... sorry ... sorry ...'

Ma put her hand on Snow's cheek. 'Why are *you* saying sorry, Xue'er?'

Snow gasped for air. She had to tell her mother, had to tell her the truth, but how did one utter those abhorrent words? How should one relay the vile misdeed committed by none other than her husband's mother?

'Xue'er, what's wrong?' Ma was beginning to worry.

With all the tumultuous energy she could muster, she blurted out a whisper, 'It was Yang's mother, Ma. It was Yang's mother. She had hit you with her sewing machine.'

Ma sat frozen for a moment, breathing heavily. Then, she slowly turned back to face the road, not uttering a word.

The two women sat side by side till darkness fell, trying to search for wisps of sanity in the rustling of the leaves as the trees greeted the evening breeze.

A week passed. Life went on. After that day, Snow and her mother did not talk about the incident. They tried to carry on with their daily activities. Snow accompanied her mother and Nenek to savour the food along Sudirman Street, where their family's restaurant was located, and to buy clothes at Jalan Cihampelas.

Every few days, there would be a phone call from Yang. He would ask after her Ma and Nenek, ask if everything was okay. Their phone conversations were short and revolved around mundane matters—her restaurant at Seah Street was doing fine, his work had been busy, he had cleaned their flat over the weekend, was she eating better now?

One evening, Ma asked Snow to sit with her in the garden. It had been two weeks since they had left Singapore. There had been a fall of rain that afternoon which drew forth a symphony of toad croaks and cricket chirps in its wake.

'You should go home soon, Xue'er.'

Ma took Snow's hand, held it in her lap. 'Maybe, it was an accident. People panic. No one would wish this on someone else,' she paused. 'Let it go. Whatever happened is not Yang's fault.'

'Ma, I know. But I need to find out.'

'You want to ask her? For what?'

Snow searched within herself for an answer to her mother's question, for an answer to her own question. All she found was three words.

'For the truth,' she said quietly.

Chapter 36

Singapore

The taxi made its way towards Bukit Ho Swee. Snow had deliberately chosen a flight arriving on a Monday morning; Yang would have to attend a routine weekly meeting with the Chief Commissioner of the SCDF and would be unable to meet her at the airport.

It was not that she did not wish to see him; in fact, whenever she heard his voice over the phone, telling her that he had gone to her restaurant—his way of saying indirectly that he missed her—she wished for his warm presence again. She missed him.

It was just that there was something that she needed to do.

She had made a phone call from the airport; his mother was at home, alone. She alighted from the taxi, carrying the *Martabak Manis* and other snacks from Bandung in one hand, pulling her suitcase along in the other.

'Ma,' she greeted when his mother opened the door. She was expecting her daughter-in-law, but was somewhat surprised at the visit directly from the airport. Snow handed her the snacks.

'My Ma bought these for you from Bandung. This pancake is very popular there, so I came straight from the airport to pass them to you.'

'Oh. *Dor tzae*, thank you,' her mother-in-law politely accepted the snacks.

Snow sat down on the sofa across from the older woman, from where she could observe her face, her eyes.

'My Ma says both of you were from the same kampong,' Snow started.

Her mother-in-law's gaze shifted from her face. 'Yes, yes,' she replied.

'The fire was terrible, wasn't it? Both you and my Ma were injured.'

The older woman glanced momentarily at her daughter-in-law, then quickly looked away. 'Yes. Terrible,' she echoed.

Snow continued, 'My Ma says she was hit by something from behind. Something like a sewing machine.'

The older woman stood up, her face turning pale. She walked to the kitchen and came back with two glasses of water, which she set down a little unsteadily on the small coffee table.

'You must be tired after the plane journey,' she said to her daughter-in-law, picking up the glass of water and sipping from it. 'Better go home and rest.'

Snow picked up her glass of water. 'It's okay, Ma. I'm not tired.'

Neither spoke for a minute as they sat drinking their water. Then, Snow looked directly into the older woman's eyes.

'Ma, do you remember what happened when you were running away from the fire?'

The water in the glass in her mother-in-law's hand jerked. 'No, no, I can't remember. Everyone was panicking. I can't remember.'

She did not meet Snow's gaze, but Snow observed the quickened breaths; saw fear in her eyes, fear which belied the guilt of a conscience that was not free.

That was, perhaps, all that Snow needed to see. She placed the glass back on the table, thanked the older woman, and took her leave. Her feet brought her down the corridor; one foot in front of the other, one step, two steps, three steps, four; her mind vaguely aware of one hand pulling her luggage, the other hand cupping her mouth, then resting on her forehead. The constriction in her chest would not ease.

She had had to put on an act, a necessary performance to call a culprit's bluff, to obtain the answer which she had come here to seek; she had come to seek the truth, a truth that now burned her in the same way the fire had burned her mother a long time ago.

That night, she looked up at the clock from where she was seated at the edge of her bed. Yang had called in the afternoon, had wanted to ensure that she was safely home after the flight; had told her that there was an urgent meeting in the evening, that he would be home late.

At 9 p.m., the gate clicked open. It was just her husband coming home from work, the way he had done each day for the past seven years; the man who had held her, loved her, stood by her in both her youth and adulthood. And yet, her heart lurched forward.

He opened the front door, walked in; placed the keys on the dining table, his eyes searching for her presence the entire time. She stepped out of their bedroom.

They stood facing the other in the living room of their home.

He gazed at her. Three weeks, and her face had grown a little thinner, her hair a little messier, her eyes swollen and puffy. He smiled at her, a smile which was in part happy, in part wistful.

She met his gaze, the gaze of the one person in this world who came as close to being her soulmate as was possible. The friend who at times argued with her, but who still accepted her as she was; the companion who was not always there, but who understood and walked with her when it mattered; the lover who at times riled her, but who, after they had made their peace, would hold her in his arms.

In the present encounter, he was one who cared deeply for her, who would cook eggs for her breakfast before he left for work; who would call to find out how she was despite her hostility; who had stood by her when she needed it the most years ago. One whom she loved and missed. One who knew the anguish she harboured in her heart, but who had not been able to reach that agony because she would not let him.

And in that instant, there was nothing more to resist. Her energy was consumed; her heart exhausted.

What had she been thinking? Why was uncovering the truth of the past so important anyway? To hell with the truth. At this moment, the man standing before her was no one's son—he was only her husband; no more, no less.

He took a few steps forward, till he was standing close, till she could feel his breath, see the intensity in his eyes. He gently took her hand, held it. He stroked her hair, pushed back a stray strand, kissed her on the forehead.

She placed her hand on his shoulder, let herself rest in his warm embrace, the embrace of one who could not be held accountable for a misdeed he did not commit. Her mother was right—it was not his fault. He had no knowledge of what had happened.

He kissed her ear. 'I was worried for you,' he whispered, 'I … missed you.'

'I missed you too,' she whispered back.

He wrapped his arms around her, kissed her tenderly. She ran her fingers through his hair, down his neck, down his chest, undoing the buttons on his shirt as she let his hands—the hands which had carried a child out of the burning flames; which had saved dozens of lives by fighting the fires which had endangered them; which had dug into the earth to save those buried beneath the collapsed building—caress her body, soothe her soul.

In those brief, beautiful moments, all was well.

She woke up with a start at 5 a.m. Sitting up, she looked around.

He lay on the bed beside her, asleep. She looked at his face in the dark; at the face which her unborn children would have resembled, had they not been left unborn.

A chill began to caress her face, her heart. She stared at him, at the son of the woman who had pushed her mother into the fire, whose malice had burned her mother's face, burned her mother's eyes, burned her mother's entire life.

She recoiled at the thought that she had, just hours ago, been so close to the man born of that woman. What had she done? How could she have seen him as only her husband, when he was also the son of a woman with a deep, dark secret? What kind of joke was life playing on her, on them?

Hysteria seized her. She ran into the shower, turned on the water, closed her eyes, felt the coldness on her head, her clothes, her skin. The face of a child, an unborn baby, appeared before her. Her mother appeared before her, screaming in pain, her hair on fire. Hostile stares of dozens of people now pointed at the disfigured face, scoffing, cringing in disgust.

All over her, inside and outside, the cold water gushed.

He opened his eyes, looked at the clock. Why was there the sound of water in the shower at 5 a.m.? He turned to find the bed beside him empty. He got up, walked towards the shower.

When he opened the door, he saw her standing in the shower, her soaked clothes clinging to her body, the cold water raining down on her. Aghast, he quickly turned off the water.

She continued standing there with her back to him, sobbing.

He grabbed a towel, wrapped it around her. Then he wrapped his arms around her, hugging her from behind.

'What's wrong?' he whispered, holding her tight. His heart ached to see her thus.

She was shivering, but her breathing gradually calmed down as he held her, as they stood there, the minutes ticking by.

'I lost our child. Again,' she finally said softly.

She fell silent. Then, with a distant look in her eyes, she went on. 'The fire. Someone saw. She told me, at the hospital. She saw your mother, saw your mother hit my mother. From behind. With her sewing machine.'

Chapter 37

The next evening, he went to his mother's place.

Snow had told him. About what the neighbour had said. What her Ma had said. What his Ma had said when Snow visited her to find out the truth. What she had not said but that Snow saw in her eyes.

He knew his Ma. His entire life, he had never heard her apologize to anyone, nor admit to any mistake or wrongdoing. Her pride would not permit it. As he grew older, he began to understand why she pushed the blame for his father's departure onto his sisters and him; why she was always critical of him and his sisters, even when—especially when—she was at fault.

She was behaving a little differently today. When he arrived, she went to the kitchen, scooped a bowl of porridge, and placed it on the table. 'For you,' she told him.

It was the peanut porridge he had grown up eating; the same porridge he had helped her sell every day outside the Pepsi factory. The thick, warm broth stirred up memories which assailed his mind, regardless of consent. In all likelihood, she had been expecting his visit; after the surprise visit by Snow, she was prepared for the questions he might ask.

'I already told your wife. I can't remember what happened. Do you know how terrible the fire was? Do you know how scared I was? Huh! You don't know!' she suddenly exclaimed.

'Then why did you go back into the fire?' he asked, trying to push back the rising heat inside. He should have known what she would say.

'Why? You want to know why?'

She grabbed his arm and pulled him into her room, pointing to the sewing machine sitting at the corner, beneath the cloth.

'Why? Because of that thing! Because that was the only thing your father ever bought for me!'

They stood there, both heaving angry breaths. He turned to look at her.

'Did you knock over anyone? When you were trying to escape?' he tried to calm down, mouthing his words slowly, clearly. 'Did … you?'

'I told you already. Everyone was running. How do I know? If they want to get in the way, it's not my fault!'

He stared at her averted face, looked into the eyes which did not dare look into his. Then he yanked the cloth covering the sewing machine and threw it down onto her bed.

'Do you know what you did?' he shouted. 'You destroyed someone's life! Do you know?'

She now looked at him angrily. 'How dare you talk to me like that? Do you know how much I've suffered? Because of you, because of all of you! Other people suffer? How about me, huh? Look at my face! Have you forgotten? You are my son! Have you forgotten?'

Their words of wrath filled the room with a long, charged silence.

He walked to the door. Then he stopped, turning back slightly, choking up.

'Ma, how am I supposed to face …' he could not complete his sentence. He shut his eyes for a few seconds, then turned and left the house.

He walked for a long time that night. He walked along the Singapore River, along the Kallang River, the sounds and the smells of the water drifting along the edges of his consciousness, neither leaving, nor entering.

He lost track of the time. The people around became fewer, the traffic on the roads thinner. Still, he walked, going nowhere in particular.

He saw again his wife standing beneath the cold shower; saw again the ruined face of her mother. The unseeing eyes. The gawking eyes and hushed murmuring of the people in the restaurant when they saw her. The shocked face of his mother when she first saw the woman she had destroyed. The anguish of the 15-year-old girl outside her provision shop in the face of hurtful words from strangers.

His mother's voice lingered on in his ears, her words ringing loud and clear in his mind. Four words wrapped their claws around him, refusing to let go.

You are my son.

He sat down on a bench, looking out over the water, not knowing or caring where he was; sat in the company of the shadows cast by the yellow, melancholy breath of the street lamps, which stood with their heads drooped, bent over as if in sorrow as they shed their tears of light, casting a pall of shadows, of regrets, over those in their embrace; over those who sought distance from the dark, whose eyes could perceive the bushes and benches and buildings presented by the light, but who had to live with a trail of darkness that always came with the light.

Shadows and regrets reeked of friendship, of complicity—they stalked a person from behind. No matter how you tried to shake them off, they always crept up from behind.

All his life, he had been fighting. And yet, it seemed that it had all come to naught. He had come full circle from the time he had sat looking out over the Kallang River eighteen years ago, the night she had seen him fighting. Perhaps, he should not have pulled her back into his life, should not have fought for her love. Time and again, in wanting to protect her, he had simply ended up hurting her.

That was the truth, as much as it was that something had happened in that fire—a secret, hidden for more than thirty years, whose sinister tremors defined the landscape of their lives now as much as they did then.

For, in the final analysis, the truth that could not be denied was as simple as a daughter not being able to deny being the daughter of her parents, and a son not being able to deny being the son of his parents.

She was asleep when he got home in the wee hours of the morning. He had a shower, then sat on the sofa, where he dozed for an hour or two, till his alarm went off at 7 a.m., after which he left for work, while she was still asleep.

For the next few days, they kept themselves busy with work, seeing little of each other. He did not mention his visit to his mother. Perhaps she had an inkling that he had asked his Ma, but she did not ask. Neither of them felt ready to broach the subject. A splinter had been thrust into the space between them, but what had happened had happened, and there was nothing they could do about it.

A week later, she got a phone call from Bandung. Nenek had suffered a fall and had fractured her hips. She was now in the hospital, with surgery to be performed. A flight back to Bandung was quickly booked, for she had to go back. Budi would have to employ additional staff at the restaurant to tide the restaurant over.

Yang accompanied her to Changi Airport. They found themselves at the viewing gallery once again.

'I've been meaning to say sorry,' he said as they stood side by side, his hands on the metal bar erected to keep people away from the glass façade. Outside, a plane took off, leaving a trail of sound from its engine.

'Say sorry on her behalf?' she replied.

He didn't know what to say.

'What did she tell you? Was it an accident?' she continued.

Again, he didn't know how to answer her question. 'She said she was scared. She panicked.'

'So, she thinks she was the only one who was scared? The only one who deserved to escape?'

'No, I didn't say that. I didn't mean that.'

'So, she knocked my Ma and Cheong Soh over with her sewing machine. Because she panicked.'

'She said everyone was running. Maybe she didn't mean to. I don't know—'

'Are you defending her?' she retorted, agitation lurking beneath the effort to stay calm. 'Then why are you saying sorry? If she didn't mean it, why are you apologizing?'

'Because whether or not it was an accident, her sewing machine hit your Ma, and I'm sorry for that. I'm sorry for what your Ma has been through. For what you've been through.'

She turned to face him, her voice becoming scathing. 'And that's it? You're saying sorry for her, and that's it? For making my Ma blind and disfigured her whole life?'

He looked at her, his eyes imploring, his muscles tensing with the mounting vexation that made his voice louder. 'What do you want me to do?'

'She won't even admit, won't even apologize, and you're defending her still?'

'I'm not defending her. She's been like that all her life. Never apologizing, never admitting any mistake.'

'The least she can do is say sorry to my Ma, and she won't even do that?'

'I can't change her,' he said matter-of-factly.

She glared at him. 'So, you're letting her just get away with it?'

Unable to keep a lid on his frustration any longer, he blurted out, 'What can I do? You want me to drag her to kneel in front of your Ma?' He met her hostile stare, and a sharp pain burned in his chest. He lowered his voice. 'I thought you understood. You know what my family is like. You know how my Ma has always treated me.'

They turned away from each other, staring instead at the vast emptiness of the runway and the field in front of them.

He had not meant it to turn out this way. She was hurting, he knew that, and he never meant to inflict more pain. In a short while, she would be boarding the plane, heading to a place hundreds of miles away. He did not know how long she would be gone this time, and he wished to hold her hand, to kiss her on the forehead before she left.

Yet, the distance between them had already begun to grow. A simmering separation had already set in. And he did not blame her, for it was his family that had wronged her family.

She picked up her bag and they walked in silence to the departure gate. He took a final look at her as he said, 'Take care of yourself.'

She nodded without looking at him. 'You too,' she said wearily. Then she headed towards the departure gate. Perhaps it was better this way, he told himself, as her figure disappeared into the distance. It would have been more painful for her to stay. A splinter pierced when enfolded in flesh; it did no harm when set free in the air.

Once again, he could only watch helplessly as she walked away, as the plane lifted her further and further from his heavy heart.

Chapter 38

1995 was ushered in and the weeks trudged along.

Nenek was in the hospital for six weeks, undergoing two operations on her fractured hips. Snow stayed on in Bandung to take care of her. Recovery was a slow and difficult process, given her age. Upon discharge from the hospital, she was barely able to walk and had to depend on her granddaughter to get through daily life.

Adjusting to his wife's absence, to living alone again, was a struggle for Yang at first. Their interactions became emails and an occasional phone call. He threw himself into his work, going home late each night. Yet, no matter how late it was when he stepped into his home, the silence, the emptiness, blew into his face like a gust of wind. No matter how easily the time passed when he was busy at work, the unslept on space on the bed beside him amplified the vacuous nights, chiding the clock into slowing the footsteps of her passage.

One night, as he lay sleepless at midnight, two months since she had left, it occurred to him that he had been remiss in not doing what he should have done much earlier. When morning came, he booked a ticket to Bandung and applied for leave from work for a week.

There was something he needed to do; something he owed to Snow, her mother, and her grandmother.

He rang the bell at the gate to the old terrace house along Jalan Sumber Mulya. The descending sunlight filtered through the trees lining the small road. The man at the makeshift stall across the road called out, 'Bakso Jawir!' He was selling the popular local dish of meatballs in broth.

Snow stepped out of the house. She stood there, astonished, when she saw him standing outside the gate. He had not told her he was coming to Bandung.

He gazed at her standing several metres from where he stood outside the gate, at the face so dear yet so distant, at the woman he had once held in his arms, whose life had now become so separate from his.

She saw the wistful smile on his face, in his eyes, as she came to open the gate.

'I took a week off work,' he told her.

She nodded in reply. He observed the fatigue on her face and in the way her hair was haphazardly pushed back by a headband. The strain of looking after her Nenek for two months. Her Ma, her uncle, and his wife got up from the dining table where they were having their dinner, walking out to greet him.

'Come and have dinner with us,' her Ma said.

After dinner, he went to Nenek's room to see her. She turned when he stepped quietly into the dimly lit room. Seeing him, she smiled. She had lost weight; her clothes hung loosely about her frail frame. The fracture would take months to heal, rendering her bedbound for much of that time.

She reached her hand out to him, and he held it. She had always been kind and nurturing towards him, like a grandmother he never had. In that moment, he admonished himself in the silence of his heart for taking such a long time before coming to see her.

'Sorry, Nenek. I should have come earlier,' he said.

She waved his apology away. '*Aiya, tidak apa*, it's okay,' she said, patting his hand with her other hand.

They chatted. After a while, she placed her hand on his arm, looking at him as she said, 'Xue'er has told me. About what happened.'

He met her gaze, then looked down.

'It's not your fault,' she continued. 'We cannot be responsible for what our parents did.'

Without looking up, he said, 'That's also why I came. To say sorry.'

She patted his arm. 'No need to say sorry. Xue'er's Ma and I don't blame you.'

He sat with her for a while longer before taking his leave. As he turned to go, he realized Snow was standing at the doorway, just outside the room.

'I came to tell you … I tidied the spare bedroom for you,' she told him a little awkwardly.

'Thanks,' he nodded.

She showed him to his room. 'Rest early, goodnight,' she smiled.

'Goodnight,' he replied, returning her smile.

In the morning, Snow's uncle, seated at the dining table having his breakfast, motioned for Yang to join him. '*Mari, makan*, come and eat. Your wife went with my wife to the market,' he said, offering Yang a slice of toast and a cup of coffee. Yang accepted the older man's hospitality, asking where Snow's Ma was. 'In the garden,' he replied, 'She often sits there.'

After breakfast, Yang went out into the garden. There was an empty rattan chair beside the one on which Ma was seated. He went up, sat beside her.

'Morning, Ma.'

She smiled when she heard his greeting. 'Morning, Yang. You slept well?'

'Yes, thanks.'

He looked at her, smiling without resentment at the son of the woman who had pushed her into the fire. She asked him about his flight, about his work. They talked about things in general—the food in Bandung, Nenek's fall.

He could feel the nervous beating of his heart—he had to find a suitable pause in their conversation to say what he had come here to say.

'Ma,' he started.

She sensed that there was something he wanted to say and listened calmly.

'I came … to say sorry. To ask for your forgiveness.'

She reached out, squeezed his hand to acknowledge what he had said.

He went on, 'What my Ma did … I'm sorry. I know whatever I say can't change anything, but, I felt, I owe you at least this.'

He glanced at her unseeing eyes, at her composure, the calmness of her demeanour. The serenity about her was of one who had suffered greatly and had managed to find her peace with the world.

'Thank you, Yang. Don't blame yourself. It's not your fault,' she said slowly, contemplatively. 'Your Ma, I think, didn't wish for this to happen too.'

They sat there, neither of them speaking for a while.

Finally, he said, 'Thank you, Ma.'

She smiled. 'Help me take care of my daughter,' she said.

Over the next few days, Yang helped Snow take care of Nenek. He helped to support her when she needed to walk to the toilet or to stretch her muscles; helped to buy the groceries, do some of the cooking and cleaning; kept Nenek and Ma company, chatting with them.

When Nenek was resting and she had a bit of time, Snow accompanied Yang around Bandung. The last time he had been here was for their wedding celebration, and they had been too busy then to visit the local places.

She took him to the well-known food haven along Sudirman Street, where her family's restaurant was located. Besides this restaurant and the one in Singapore, her family owned a restaurant in Jakarta as well. They shopped at Jalan Cihampelas, where she bought him a few shirts and they bought new curtains for their flat. They bought baked banana pastry, the ones Nenek loved, from the famous Kartika Sari Pastry Shop. Nenek's eyes lit up when she saw the snack. '*Sedap*, delicious,' she mumbled as she munched on the fragrant pastry.

The day before he was to leave, they had dinner at a café on the hills in the Dago area, overlooking the city lights. They stood at the edge of the café, looking out at the luminous landscape before them, breathing in the light wind brushing against their cheeks.

She turned, smiled at him. 'Thank you, for coming. For …' She wanted to say, 'For saying sorry to Ma and Nenek', but the words seemed to get caught on the thorns on the stems which gave rise to them.

His affectionate gaze took in her smile, took in the sight of her hair being blown into a mess by the wind. How did one hold on to a smile and never let it go; to a beautiful moment that would slip by all too soon?

He reached out and took her hand. She let her hand rest in his. They stood there, hand in hand.

Chapter 39

Snow stayed on in Bandung for another two months. When Nenek was able to walk with the aid of a walking frame, she returned to Singapore.

Life went on. For a time, Snow did not accompany Yang on his visits to his mother. Their last encounter was when Snow had attempted to draw out the truth from her; even then, despite the months that had passed, she found herself becoming agitated at the mere thought of coming face to face with the older woman.

One day, Dai Kah Jie called to say that Ma was in the hospital. She had had a headache for two days and had called for an ambulance herself. When Yang told Snow, she said, 'I'll go with you.'

They rushed to the hospital. Dai Kah Jie met them along the corridor outside Ma's ward, on her way to get something to eat. 'The doctor had said that it was nothing serious and had prescribed some painkillers,' Dai Kah Jie told them. 'Just a bad headache, the doctor had said.'

Ma did not see Yang and Snow as they entered the ward. She was using the hospital telephone, talking, presumably to a friend, in quite her usual fashion when she gossiped for hours over the phone at home. When she caught sight of them, she hurriedly put the phone down, lay on the bed in an ailing manner, and spoke with a feeble voice.

Yang exchanged glances with Snow. 'She seems fine,' Snow muttered. Yang sighed, whether in relief or exasperation Snow could not quite tell. Probably both.

Snow kept her composure as she sat on the chair beside the hospital bed, with Yang standing beside her. She watched incredulously as Ma spoke in a deliberately frail manner. '*Hou tong ah, ngor meng hou fu ah!* Very painful ah, my life has so much suffering!'

That night, Snow had trouble sleeping. Till now, there had been no indication whatsoever of regret on the part of his Ma, of being sorry for what she had done to her Ma, even if she had not meant it. That was perhaps what hurt the most. There was no attempt to confront what she had done, to look truth in the face, to feel sorry for the harm her selfish actions had caused, and to express remorse. To her, she had done nothing wrong. She pretended as if nothing had happened at all.

Over the next few weeks, Snow and Yang had many arguments. After being discharged from the hospital, his Ma would call him every day, asking in a weak voice if he could buy her some food after work. Snow insisted that there was nothing wrong with her, that she was not really sick, but Yang still did what his Ma asked him to do.

'She's using emotional blackmail. Feigning sickness so you feel guilty if you don't go. Can't you tell?' she asked curtly.

'She's getting old,' he replied.

'She's pretending! Can't you see? Just like she's been pretending nothing happened in the fire!' she snapped.

He kept silent. She started to get agitated.

'Aren't you going to say anything? Have you forgotten? Just because we don't talk about it, you conveniently forgot? She's pretending so she doesn't have to say sorry!'

He searched for the words he should say, for he really did not know what he should be saying. Finally, staring into the empty space ahead, he said, 'That's why I apologized, on her behalf.'

The vexation and resentment inside erupted, and she flew off the handle. 'That's not the same! You're not the one who pushed my Ma into the fire!'

'I know and I'm sorry for what happened. You know that! How many times have I said sorry? Why can't you put it behind you? Why must you keep bringing it up? What do you want me to do?' he flared up, his anger and frustration bursting as he hit his fist against the wall. 'She's my mother. What can I do about that? Whatever I say or do can't change the fact that I'm her son!'

His words seared her heart, the way the words of the person closest to you would when they revealed that he did not understand you at all; when they revealed that he was not on your side after all.

A fiery beast reared its appalling head, and he slammed his fist repeatedly against the wall. 'You shouldn't have married me in the first place! It was a mistake, wasn't it?'

She stood there helplessly, staring at the stranger she had married; at the angry man who was the son of a depraved woman. She shut her eyes, clenched her fists. Then, she walked away.

Three days later, he apologized for what he had said, as did she. They tried to speak in a civil manner, in a cordial manner. They attempted to get along, to get on with life. They struggled by in this manner in the ensuing months.

At the same time, Nenek's health, which had taken a turn for the worse ever since her hip fracture, began to deteriorate, with recurring urinary tract infections which required repeated courses of antibiotics, frequent bouts of influenza, and a poor appetite.

Snow had to shuttle back and forth between Singapore and Bandung; back and forth she and Yang swung between arguments and patching up.

Then, the 1997 Asian financial crisis struck.

Chapter 40

Thailand, Indonesia, Malaysia, and other Asian countries reeled from the collapse of their currencies, the flight of investors from the region, and the precipitous drop in asset prices. The crisis, which started with the slump of the Thai Baht in July 1997, quickly spread across the region, leading to an economic meltdown in most Southeast Asian countries.

Singapore was not spared the spillover effects of the fallout. The economy took a battering and companies shuttered or downsized along with the erosion of confidence in the region.

With significant business investments in Singapore and Malaysia, Ah Pui's fortunes tumbled as debt piled up. Profit plummeted. Banks pulled back credit lines as the value of assets and collaterals dropped.

The possibility of going bankrupt loomed large for Ah Pui. When Yang met him for dinner one evening, he was struck by how Ah Pui's shirt hung more loosely than it usually did—Ah Pui had shed more weight in those few months than he did in their decades-long friendship.

Desperate, he asked Yang for whatever financial help he could get. Having had a stable job, Yang had built up some savings. Through all their years of friendship, Ah Pui had never asked to borrow money from Yang, till this crisis. Yang lent Ah Pui $20,000. Though not substantial compared to the hundreds of thousands of snowballing debts, Yang helped, in his small way, his friend to tide over the crisis.

Snow's family business was hit as well, with the plummeting of the Indonesian Rupiah and the consequent soaring of prices in Indonesia. Their restaurant business was battered, though their family's longstanding belief in low leveraging served them well in staving off the escalating debt faced by many other businesses.

All this while, Nenek's health continued its decline. Snow was in Indonesia often, helping to take care of Nenek as well as their restaurants in Bandung and Jakarta. In Singapore, Budi was able to manage the restaurant, steering it through the crisis which was not as severe in Singapore as it was in Indonesia.

While the financial and economic meltdown took its toll, what battered Snow's family and many others in Indonesia was something else. What was set in motion by the financial and economic woes was a human catastrophe none of them had foreseen.

In May 1998, riots broke out throughout Indonesia, mainly in Jakarta, Medan, and Solo. Food shortages and mass unemployment led to demonstrations and violence. In Jakarta, thousands of students marched in protest, clashing with the police. Shots were fired. In the ensuing chaos, four students were killed.

Mass violence and unrest followed. Angry mobs torched buildings. Properties owned by Chinese Indonesians became common targets. Jakarta's Chinatown was badly damaged. Throughout Indonesia, hundreds of lives were lost, and more than a hundred cases of rape were reported; women and girls, many of them Chinese, were raped. Many Indonesian Chinese fled to Singapore, China, and Australia, never returning.

Snow was in Bandung during this time. Nenek was very ill and bedridden at home, fighting a bout of pneumonia. Although Bandung was not as badly afflicted as Jakarta, nevertheless, there were incidents of violence and unrest. In the face of her Nenek's illness and with the threat of violence and rape ever present, Snow felt as alone and afraid as ever.

One day, when the violence in Jakarta was especially intense, she and her family received the news that their restaurant in Jakarta had been torched, along with neighbouring shops and restaurants, by arsonists and looters. They, too, had fallen victim to the riots. They also heard that a young woman, who worked in a shop adjacent to their restaurant, had been raped.

Snow and her family partitioned a small room at the back of their house as an emergency hiding place, with a door separating the room from the main house and another door at the back to run away if violence reached their house.

One afternoon, they heard shouts outside. 'Quick! Go to the room at the back!' her uncle cried out. Snow, her Ma, and her uncle's wife scurried to the room at the back, where they crouched and waited with bated breath, huddling in fear. They hid for what seemed like a long time, not daring to talk, not daring to go to the toilet. It was over an hour later when her uncle came to tell them that it was safe to go back into the house.

She, her Ma, and her aunt cut their hair short, as short as a boy's haircut. They wore hats. They wore her uncle's clothes. They did not dare venture out of the house. They did not even dare stand close to the windows, afraid that people could see them from the outside. Her uncle had to go out to get food and other necessities, and they made do with whatever they had in the house.

When the violence finally died down, the destruction—human destruction as much as it was economic and political—was colossal. Cataclysmic and tragic. President Suharto resigned. Vice President Habibie took over the presidency. The trauma of the violence and rapes continued to haunt those who lived through it for years to come.

During the days of the riots, Yang had wanted to fly over to Bandung. He was worried for Snow and her family. He should have gone over to protect her and her family.

But he didn't. He was held back by responsibilities at work. His job was in Singapore. His life was in Singapore. And he was held back by the need to care for his mother, who had just been diagnosed with nose cancer, requiring aggressive treatment.

He could only remain on the sidelines of Snow's life, helpless, as she fought her own battles far away, as she soldiered on with her own life, alone. It was as if they now lived separate lives.

Chapter 41

On 20 June 1998, a month after the resignation of President Suharto, Nenek passed away.

Yang flew to Bandung for the funeral. He stood with Snow and her Ma, in their boys' haircut, as they sent Nenek off. Each grieving, and each alone in their grief.

Snow returned to Singapore with Yang after the funeral. She visited his Ma in the hospital after her chemotherapy treatment. She tried to support her when she was too weak to walk. She tried to ignore the lingering resentment she felt towards her, buried deep inside. As she held his Ma's hand, she tried to push away the memories of her own mother feeling her own way through the sudden blindness that had beset her.

She started having nightmares; started suffering from insomnia. The nights brought her back to the horror of the riots, to the terror they felt as they cut one another's hair, to the cowering in the room behind their house when they heard shouts on the streets, to Ma's helplessness, being blind, in the face of the violence outside, to Nenek's face as she lay dying on her bed. In her dreams she saw Yang's mother, hugging her sewing machine and laughing. She saw Yang standing beside his mother. She heard the scoffs and hushed whispers of unseen people. She heard her Ma crying alone in the garden. She heard her unborn child crying.

The number of medicines in her list of medications drawer grew. She tried to manage on her own. The amount of time she and Yang spent together dwindled, as he tried to juggle work and taking care of his Ma as she underwent treatment. At times, an entire week would pass with the two of them hardly seeing each other, hardly exchanging a word.

Yang knew of his wife's nightmares, her troubled sleep. She had woken up often in middle of the night, and he had only been able to sit beside her on the bed, helpless. With his responsibilities at work and in taking care of his Ma continuing relentlessly, he found himself sleeping through her nightmares and insomnia more easily, more frequently, as he lay in bed, his energy spent.

Late one night, he entered their bedroom quietly. Still in his work clothes, he sat on the bed, gazed at the sleeping figure of the woman he had loved all his life. He wanted to reach out to touch her cheek, to hold her hand, to caress her hair. But he did not. He did not want to interrupt the little sleep she managed to catch. He did not know if she would draw away from his touch.

Perhaps, the distance between them had grown too great. Just as he had remained on the sidelines of her life, of her struggles, she too now remained on the sidelines of his life.

She knew that he was not having an easy time either. He had to take care of his ailing mother and come home to a troubled wife, over and above managing the fire rescue operations of the country. When she lay awake in the night, she looked at his sleeping figure, at the scar on his neck, at the interspersed white hair which now laced his sideburns. They had been through so much together.

And as she gazed at him, there was a burn in her heart. She knew that she cared deeply for him. Yet, she was unable to walk beside him in his life now, just as he had been unable to walk beside her in these past years.

Perhaps, they were just tired. Love had worn them down, as it had built them up before. Life had separated their paths, as it had brought them together before.

Beginnings and endings were not opposite ends of a long, straight line after all; they were not far apart from one another, not two ends of a long tunnel that you could crawl into from one side and come out of in a completely different land. They seemed more like opposite ends of an incomplete circle, as if, after pulling yourself through a great distance in a meandering tunnel, you simply emerged across the river, realizing that you had reached the end, an end that seemed so close to the beginning.

Often, two lives touched in love's encounter but found they could not embrace; each could behold the other, yet were separate; intimate, yet alone.

Chapter 42

On a wet, December night, Snow sat on the sofa at their home, listening to the soft splatter of the raindrops on the windows. She stood up, ran her hands along the smooth fabric of the curtains, fabric which they had bought during the week he had spent with her in Bandung. She walked slowly to the kitchen, running her hands across the wood of the kitchen cabinets which held in their bosom the plates and bowls they had shared, the mugs which had held coffee they had sipped on relaxed mornings together, the frying pan they had hovered over as they competed to see whose scrambled eggs tasted better.

The front door closed quietly. She stepped out of the kitchen, into the dining area where he now stood. Their gazes met, as it had countless times in the years they had spent together. She looked at his tired face, at the sadness in his eyes, and she wanted to tear the air ticket to Bali now sitting in her bag.

After the riots had destroyed her family's restaurant in Jakarta, they had decided to set up a restaurant in the tourist district of Kuta in Bali, where Snow's cousin, Budi's sister, had worked for several years. In Bali, the culture was inclusive, the people accepting and welcoming. She had chosen to run their Bali restaurant. To live in Bali. She would be leaving Singapore for Bali later that night.

He gazed at his wife, at the dark circles around her eyes, eyes that had once sparkled, but now only showed weariness. She had talked to him a week ago about going to Bali, had asked for his blessings. 'Can we give each other some time, some space?' she had asked. He did not understand what that meant. Was she asking for a separation? He had wanted to ask, but he realized that, perhaps, she did not know either. And, perhaps, at this moment, he would rather leave the question mark there. Life had taught him that often, we had to go on living without complete understanding. Uncertainty left room in her dwelling for hope; certainty did not.

Perhaps, all they knew was that he had a duty to walk with his mother as she fought for her life, regardless of what she had done in that life; that they were both struggling, hurting in their own separate ways; that she needed the time and space to heal which she could not find while her life remained here.

He took a few steps towards her. In the past five years, she had left for Bandung many times, and it had not been easy; but this time, it was different. He did not know if she would be leaving his life for good. An acute, desperate fear gripped his entire being, not unlike the despair he had felt at the river on that long-ago night when she had left his life for what was to be nine long years.

He reached out as she stood against the wall, running his hand along the contours of her face. The muscles in his face, his body, began to tense. His jaws tightened; his breathing beginning to sputter. The tension radiated into his arms, and his fist hit out at itself against the wall behind her, behind them, as he stood facing her, almost embracing, his eyes shut in anguish, his forehead touching hers.

'Sorry,' she whispered in his ear.

A tear rolled down his cheek. She put her hand to his face, wiped the tear away. He pulled her towards him, placed his cheek against hers, held her in his arms.

'No. *I'm* sorry,' he replied, holding her head against his shoulders, his tears caressing her hair.

He then gathered himself, looking at her as he held her gently by the shoulders.

'If you need me, you know where I am,' was all he could say, all he could do, as she slipped out of his life once again.

At 5 a.m., her plane took off for Bali. He stood in the viewing gallery, staring into the empty sky long after the plane had soared high above the clouds. Then he turned and walked away slowly.

The following day, the world celebrated as people everywhere bade farewell to the 20th century. Clapping and cheering, they ushered in the 21st century. A millennium had ended, and a new one was beginning.

Part Five

Spirit

Light and life gifted by the sun
Yet scars are overflowing
Washing the parched land
Into brave, lonely seas
Earth, poisoned abundance
Cries out in song
The air beckons
Courage's scent rises
Spirit
Calls from the deep

***

2002

Chapter 43

Bali, Indonesia, 2002.

The young Australian couple waved goodbye as they left the restaurant, about to make their way to the Sari Club just down the road. Snow looked up from where she was clearing the table with Komala, the local staff who'd been working at the restaurant since it opened over two years ago. They returned the couple's cheerful farewell.

After she and Komala had done the necessary clearing and cleaning, they locked the doors; bade one another goodnight. Snow glanced at her watch; it was just past 10 p.m. She strolled towards Kuta Bay, the way she had often done in the two years she'd been living here.

The crowds which buzzed on the beach during the day had thinned out along with the light of the sun, having made a beeline through the evening for the town and its nightlife. Groups of tourists remained, their laughter and chatter floating in the breeze. Several couples walked hand in hand at the edge of the sea where the water washed upon the sand. Few stood alone like her.

Her days on this island of peace-loving people had gone by peaceably. A certain measure of calm had returned to her life, with the retreat of the tumultuous emotions which had once beset her. There was a rhythm to her life whose beat, though muted, dull even, restored a sense of balance in her spirit. She often held Yang and her Ma in her thoughts, in the silence of her heart, as she stood facing the wilderness of the ocean in the still of night. She missed them, and at times a chilly loneliness gripped her. But, as she had learnt, oftentimes life rendered it necessary to be alone; it was the only way to search for yourself once again.

The ocean breathed freely upon her as she stood facing the vast expanse of water, her long hair, her flowing skirt fluttering in the wind which held in its drift the distinct smell of sea salt. She dialled the number on her mobile to reach Bandung, to reach her Ma, wanting to hear Ma's voice as much as to let Ma listen to the voice of the ocean.

'Ma, listen. The sea,' she whispered, an ache blowing in the vastness separating mother and daughter. Su Mei leaned into the phone, listened intently, gratefully, to the beauty of the water, of the wind, of her daughter's heart; two lonely women holding the lovely sea between them.

She stayed on along the beach after the call, her gaze lingering on another number on her phone, the mighty ocean lingering on her feet, then pulling away. They had continued to stay in touch largely through emails, phone messages, and occasional phone calls. He would make it a point to call her on special occasions—when she had first arrived, on their birthdays, on Christmas, New Year. And yes, on their wedding anniversary.

She wondered how he was, wondered if he would have wanted to listen to the song of the sea. Perhaps. Or perhaps not. She could no longer be certain. She knew from their emails and phone messages that his Ma was very ill. The cancer had spread. What should she say if she called him? Should she offer to go back to see his Ma?

Till this day, his Ma had continued to deny all responsibility for what had happened in the fire. By pretending that she had done nothing wrong, by not acknowledging to others as well as to herself the harm caused by her selfish actions, by insisting that she was the victim, by hiding the truth in the dark recesses of her subconscious—she absolved herself of any misdeed.

Snow placed her phone back in her handbag, turned, made her way home.

Chapter 44

Solo, Indonesia.

In a house, a group of men gathered. They huddled over a map of Bali, one of them pointing to a place on the map, giving instructions to the others. There was a new strategy, he said. They would no longer target embassies and other such prominent sites. Now, the plan was to strike soft targets. Nightclubs, bars, places where ordinary people gathered.

'Why Bali?' the man standing beside him had asked. Because it was frequented by Americans and their associates, was the reply. This was part of Jihad, holy war, to defend the people of Afghanistan from America.

This was the plan, the man went on. To detonate a small bomb in Paddy's Bar in the Kuta area. The resulting panic would send dozens of people out onto the street, where a second, much larger bomb would await them, outside the Sari Club. A third bomb would be placed near the US and the Australian Consulates. All this would be done on a Saturday night, when the area would be bustling with people, when the attack would cause the greatest devastation, when the strike on the enemy would be the most painful.

The men around the table listened, fiery resolution burning in their eyes. Yes. They would kill and be killed. They had been told that this was the ultimate honour and glory—to save the world by eradicating those who were evil; to be willing to sacrifice their own lives in this holy war.

Chapter 45

Singapore.

The tubes attached to her body rose and fell along with her laboured breath. Yang, Dai Kah Jie, and Yee Kah Jie stood beside her bed. The doctors had told them that this was the final stretch.

In the past months, Ah Feng had looked at herself in the mirror as the cancer spread, as the tumours clawed their way across her face, merrily replicating themselves on her nose, in her mouth, on her face, with no regard for her pride.

Now barely able to speak, she looked at her children, gathered around her. She looked first at Dai Kah Jie, shifted her gaze to Yee Kah Jie, and then to Yang, who met her gaze. He wanted to say something, but was tossing the thought around in his mind.

Mother and son continued to look at each other. Finally, he said, 'Ma, I'm going to make a phone call to Bandung. To Su Mei, Xue'er's Ma.'

She shifted her eyes away from her son; kept still for a long while. Then she nodded.

He dialled the number. Snow's uncle picked up the phone. He asked to speak to her Ma. His Ma looked at him, her eyes watchful. After a minute or so, Su Mei was on the phone. He explained that they were at the hospital, that his Ma's cancer had spread, that she was barely able to speak now. He asked if it was okay for him to put his Ma on the phone. There was a short pause as Su Mei took in all that he had said. Then she said yes, of course. He held the phone to his Ma's ear.

Su Mei pressed the phone to her ear. For a while there was only the sound of breathing coming through the phone receiver.

'Ah Feng,' she began, speaking in Cantonese, 'I know you can't talk. It's okay.'

She paused. The breathing became a little louder. The two women listened through the telephone pressed to their ears, listened to the sadness in their hearts for everything in their lives that could have been, but that was not, to the sound of regret flowing through their wordless breath.

'Ah Feng, I don't blame you anymore, for what happened. I wish you peace.'

Ah Feng's lips began to quiver. Yang and his sisters looked on as authentic, genuine tears started to flow down their Ma's cheeks—it was the first time they had seen their Ma cry so openly, so honestly, so unpretentiously.

Su Mei listened to the sound of Ah Feng crying. There was nothing more that needed to be said. What had to be done was now done.

Later, as Yang sat with Dai Kah Jie in the corridor of the hospital, they spoke of how Ma had never revealed much about her own parents. Yang and his sisters had never seen their grandparents. Ma only said that they had passed on by the time Dai Kah Jie was born. Dai Kah Jie told Yang that she had once overheard

Ma telling a friend over the phone that Ma's own father had left her and her mother when she was young. That her mother had passed away when she was only sixteen. 'Maybe, that's why she puts up a front all the time,' Dai Kah Jie said with a sigh.

The next day, on 25 August 2002, a month after she turned 73, Ma breathed her last.

The funeral was simple, with the wake lasting just three days. Yang's colleagues came. Ah Pui and other friends came. Dai Kah Jie's and Yee Kah Jie's friends came. They had few relatives, and Ma had few friends. Many of the neighbours, who had come to know of her barbed gossip about them, did not come.

Yang did not inform Snow and her Ma. He had been in a dilemma as to whether to do so. Legally, they were still married, and she was still his wife. But he knew that their two-year separation was due in large part to his Ma, to what she had done in the past, and to what she did not do to heal that past. To inform his wife would have been to shove the dilemma into her arms. She would have felt obliged to fly back for the funeral, but it might rekindle the pain she had been trying so hard to let go of.

Two weeks later, he received a letter from Snow's Ma. She had asked Snow's uncle to write it, after she had spoken to his Ma. It read:

'Dear Yang,

Thank you for calling me from the hospital. I am grateful, because it allowed your Ma and me to put the past behind us at last. With this, I hope you and Xue'er can also put the past behind.

I have not been able to see with my eyes, so I have learnt to see with my heart. Whatever your Ma has done is not your fault. You have been good to Xue'er, to our family. I gave you and Xue'er my blessings on your wedding day. My blessings are still with you now.

I am growing older each day, and sometimes my health is not so good. The only thing, the only person I find difficult to let go of in this world is my daughter. Please help me take care of her. Take care of each other. She still loves you.

You have always been a fighter. You have fought for others. Now fight for the love you have held on to for so long. Fight for the person you love. Don't give up on your marriage. Go to Bali. Look for her.'

Love,
Ma

He sat on the bed with the letter in his hand, alone in the home he used to share with Snow.

Two years. It had been two difficult years, with the demands placed on him by his Ma and her illness, by his work and his responsibilities, calling upon a space within him which seemed almost void. Hollow. The strain had, at times, pushed him to breaking point.

All this while, she, too, had been living alone in Bali. Many a quiet night he had wanted to call her, just as anyone would call the person he loved, to say nothing in particular and for no particular reason, other than to hear her voice. But he did not. He could no longer be sure if she would have wanted him to call; if she still kept him in her heart; if she still loved him as he loved her, or at least as he thought he loved her—for what it meant to love someone when you carried on living separate lives month after month, he did not know. It seemed as though the older he grew, the less he knew.

He sat in the impersonal space of his own bedroom, the letter from her Ma clutched in his hand, the suppressed strain, the subdued emotions of two years, in his clenched jaws, in his shut eyes. Perhaps not for nothing had he come this far. Perhaps, despite the weariness that had pervaded his spirit, there was, as her Ma urged, one more battle to fight, a fight which, at this moment, he wondered if there was pluck enough left in him to take on.

Maybe, just maybe, there was hope yet.

Chapter 46

Bali, Indonesia.

In early September, Snow received a letter from her mother. During her time in Bali, she and Ma often wrote to each other. The letters were written in braille, which she had learnt to read since young.

'My dearest Xue'er,

It was so good to hear your voice that night, when you called me from Kuta Beach. Thank you for giving me the gift of the ocean, for letting me listen to the sounds of the waves, the wind. Just like how you gave me the sounds of the river long ago.

Everything here in Bandung is well. I have been having a flu lately, but I am recovering, so don't worry. Hope everything in Bali is fine.

Yang called me from the hospital a few days ago. His mother was dying. He put her on the phone with me. Her cancer had spread all over, and she couldn't talk. I told her that I don't blame her anymore for what happened. I wished her peace.

She was silent for a while. Then I heard her crying. I could hear her regret, her sorrow, in her tears. And with her heartfelt tears, we have made peace with the past.

This would not have been possible if Yang didn't call me. I know you asked me before, why life has played such a cruel joke on us, for you to marry the son of the woman who made me blind and disfigured. Maybe, there is a reason. If not for him, I could not have been on the phone with her before her last breath. There would have been no closure. What his mother has owed to me, and to you, he has tried to repay. What misdeeds his mother committed during the fire, maybe unknowingly, he has tried to redeem, by saving lives from fires all these years. The past cannot be undone, and I guess all we can do is to try and make good with what little we have left in our small, broken lives. What more can we do, except to try?

So, my dear daughter, let's try to let it go. If you and Yang stay apart because of what happened to me, I will not have peace. I know both of you still care deeply for each other. If he looks for you, go home with him. Don't give up on him. Don't give up on the love you've shared with him all these years.

You have been the greatest blessing to me in my life. I wish for you to be happy, and I love you always.

Love,
Ma

She ran her fingers along the little dots on the page, touching the love conveyed by her Ma through them. Yang's Ma may have passed away, since Yang had called her Ma days ago, as Ma mentioned in her letter. She had known that this moment would soon come, yet now that it had come, she did not know what to feel, if such a thing as knowing what to feel was possible at all. Perhaps, she ought to feel sad—wasn't it only proper to feel sad now that the woman who had given life to her husband had gone? There was a measure of sadness, am indistinct ache in the heart. But there was also a vague sense of relief, as if a sharp weight was being lifted, pushing its way through. She closed her eyes. A thick numbness seemed to wrap itself around her.

The moment when the past could be buried had finally come, the time when the struggles of many, brought upon by the selfishness of one, could be laid to rest. And as she sat in the solitude of her room with her mother's letter in her hand, the healing tears came at last.

A week later, she received a text message from Yang.

'Hope you are well. Ma has passed away. I thought of informing you earlier but decided not to. Didn't want to put you in a difficult position. I put Ma on the phone with your Ma before she went. My duty as a son is now done. Can I come to Bali in a few weeks to see you? I have to settle Ma's affairs and tie up some loose ends at work. After that, I will book a flight to Bali. With love, Yang.'

In western Java, another part of the country, a group of men convened for a meeting, the same men who had met a few weeks ago in Solo to discuss their mission in Bali.

They were informed that the Bali attack was originally planned for 11 September 2002, to mark the first anniversary of the terror attacks on the US. The bombs, however, were not ready. Their plans had to be postponed.

Chapter 47

Yang arrived in Bali on the afternoon of Saturday, 12 October 2002. He got into a taxi at Ngurah Rai International Airport, asking the driver to take him to the Ramayana Hotel in Kuta. He checked into the hotel, freshened up before making his way to Jalan Legian, the street where Snow's restaurant was located.

The evening sunlight was slanting in by the time he strode towards Jalan Legian. He stopped for a moment, hesitating. It had been more than two years since he last saw her. In reply to his text message informing her of his Ma's passing and asking if he could come to see her, she had said, 'Sorry to hear about your Ma. Thank you for calling my Ma. You are welcome to come to Bali any time. Yours, Xue'er.'

He had read her message many times over, trying to decipher the emotions in her words and between her words. In the end, he gave up. These were polite words one might write to any friend, and there was no way to decode the emotions embodied, or rather not embodied, in them. He just had to take the risk in coming, the way he had taken the risk each time he approached a fire.

There it was. Her restaurant. His steps slowed down; his pulse quickened. He stood outside in the same way he had stood outside her restaurant in Singapore years ago. He peered in.

There she was—chatting cheerfully with a Caucasian couple at a table. She looked a little older, as did he, and had put on a little weight. Her eyes were as genuine as ever. She seemed happy, exuding the spirited charm he'd always been drawn to.

He stepped in; she looked up. Her eyes met his intense gaze; she looked at the man who was still her husband, but whom she had not seen for over two years. She was expecting his arrival; nonetheless she had to put down the plate she was carrying, for it seemed to be tremoring with nervousness. For a moment, neither of them spoke; neither knew what to say, how to greet the other—what first words ought to be uttered between lovers who'd been apart for so long?

'Welcome to Bali,' she blurted out, regretting what she'd said immediately. What was with her, greeting him as if a stranger, as if a tourist who'd just walked into her restaurant? She tried again. 'You just arrived?' That was a little better, perhaps.

He nodded. 'Yes, just this afternoon,' he replied. He looked around at the place packed with people of all nationalities. There were Caucasians—probably Australians and Americans—as well as Japanese and Singaporeans. A young Indonesian lady was helping to serve the customers. She must be Komala, he thought, recalling Snow mentioning the Indonesian waitress who had been helping her these past two years.

He did not know what else to say; the place was teeming with customers. 'You must be busy. What time do you close?'

'Saturday nights are always busy. We close around 11 p.m.'

'I'll come back later then.'

He smiled awkwardly; as did she.

In Bandung, Su Mei sat in the garden on this dusk of 12 October. The softening light of the sun had brought with it a gentle fall of rain. She listened to the patter of the water on the soil of their garden, on the earth which had nourished the mango tree planted by her daughter when they first came to live in Bandung, gifting them with the richness of mangoes over the years. The scent of the mangoes, now hanging amid the abundant foliage, met her unseen breath.

She lifted her blind eyes to the heavens, eyes that, having been denied their outward gaze, had learnt to turn inwards to the inner spirit, and through the eyes of that spirit gaze again upon the world. Often, that spirit was simply the love between two persons, between a man and a woman, between a mother and her child; love that was as deep as it was inexplicable.

She saw again the faces of her parents, her husband, her mother-in-law, all of whom were now with her only in spirit. She imagined the face of her daughter, the grown woman whom she had only been able to see as a baby, the one person in this world whose life mattered more to her than anything else, who had told her that she was looking forward to Yang's visit. Yang had also written, in response to her letter, saying that he would look for her daughter in Bali, that he would take care of her.

With this, she was at peace. Her life seemed complete, with no regrets holding her back.

Yet, she seemed to feel a vague sense of unease. She could not put a finger to it, other than it being the sense of an undefined darkness, as if some danger lurked somewhere. As she sat beneath the setting sun and the light fall of rain, breathing the air scented by the rich earth, she lifted a silent prayer to the heavens.

Her spirit called upon the power of the universe, the redemptive spirit of goodness; reaching out, touching the universal suffering of the world—her share of which she had borne with quiet acceptance in her own solitary life—and becoming one with the cosmos of which her own spirit was merely a part.

She stood for a time, and peace once again came to rest in her heart. Night had fallen around her, as had a weariness in her body.

Later that night, she picked up the telephone, dialled the number to her daughter's mobile phone. It rang, but her daughter did not pick it up. She was probably busy at the restaurant.

She waited for a while, then tried again. Still, there was no answer.

Chapter 48

The town of Kuta, Bali, was a hive of people and activity late into the night.

Yang explored the sights and sounds of the area as he waited till Snow's restaurant could close its doors for the day. He stood at Kuta beach overlooking Kuta Bay. He walked along the streets, identified the famous Sari Club. He visited the Kuta night market, where crowds gathered to catch glimpses of the famous Luwak—the small, nocturnal civet native to Bali and parts of Asia—after which the exotic Luwak coffee was named, deriving its peculiarity from the coffee beans collected after being eaten and excreted by these civets.

Yang found himself basking in the warmth and hospitality of the Balinese Indonesians. They were, as Snow had mentioned many a time, genuinely friendly and helpful. A young, local boy with an impish grin carried a stool over to him after he had stood at the same place for a time, not knowing where else to go.

At 11 p.m., amid the hubbub of locals and tourists from all around the world, a man walked into Paddy's Bar, along

Jalan Legian, with explosives hidden in his backpack. At about the same time, another man driving a white minivan loaded with explosives pulled up to the sidewalk outside the Sari Club, opposite Paddy's Bar.

Within a few minutes, as yet unknown to everyone else on the island and the rest of the world, Bali would be changed forever, its history and culture henceforth stained with the blood of innocent lives.

Yang made his way back towards Jalan Legian at about 11 p.m., marvelling at the throngs making their way towards the Sari Club two hundred metres away.

Suddenly, a loud crack rang through the air, not unlike the sound of firecrackers. Seconds later, blood-curdling screams sliced the night as blood-smeared people ran out of Paddy's Bar. Yang and all those around him stood aghast.

Then, the earth shook as a massive ball of fire roared into existence outside the Sari Club, swallowing human bodies and vehicles alike in its fiery hunger. Seismic equipment in Bali recorded vibrations which were felt over a 20 km radius and registered 0.2 on the Richter scale. The sound was heard at the airport, four kilometres away.

Windows shattered, spewing their glass shards into the air, into the buildings, into the bodies of people all around. Metal and wood flew like a thousand misfired darts, shooting at lightning speed into human flesh and non-human objects in their path. People were ripped apart. Hands and legs were sliced. The Sari Club moaned loudly as its roof and body collapsed onto hundreds of helpless humans. Buildings around it crumpled and fell.

Yang was thrown off the ground by a powerful gust of hot air. When he sat up, he saw the people around him similarly on the ground. Many started getting up, their faces covered in shock and dust. Farther down the road, a large inferno blazed where the Sari Club used to stand. Most of the people nearer the inferno did not get up from the ground. Some lay motionless on top of others. Glass and metal and wood and blood were strewn all over the ground, along with parts of bodies—arms and legs which had belonged to living, breathing people just minutes ago. In all his years as a firefighter, he had never seen such devastation.

A sharp pain shot up his leg. When he looked down, he saw blood mushrooming down his jeans. There was a long gash on his left leg, just above his knee, in which a shard of glass was embedded, part of it jutting out. His arms were peppered with lacerations. Shrapnel wounds. With his hands and his right leg, he heaved himself up.

An Australian man beside him asked, 'You okay, mate?'

He replied, 'Yeah. You?' He saw that the man had cuts on his face and hands.

The man put his hands to his head as they stared in disbelief at the carnage around them. 'Some cuts here and there. But we're lucky. Just look at that. Oh, bloody hell!'

'Bom! Bom!' two local men exclaimed, pointing towards the Sari Club. They started running in the direction of the large blaze.

Yang jolted as awareness of what had just happened began sinking in. *Oh no. Snow*, he thought, his body almost going numb as the horror of what could have happened to her stared him in the face.

Her restaurant was further up the road from the Sari Club. He hobbled as quickly as he could through the sea of glass and stone, wood and metal, dismembered hands and legs. Dead bodies.

As he neared the Sari Club, he heard people shouting for help. There were people trapped in the fire. Many of them. He couldn't just walk past; he had to help. The two local men he had seen earlier were pulling a woman out of the wreckage. They put her at the back of a pickup truck, and one of them took the wheel to get her to the hospital.

Yang pushed into the familiar, intense heat of the fire as he entered the collapsed, burning building. Several locals and tourists, including the Australian he'd spoken to earlier, were in there trying to help the trapped victims. A woman trapped beneath wooden beams, a few metres in, looked at them. 'Help me,' she cried out.

Together with the Australian, Yang navigated carefully through the flames to reach the woman. There were hollow spaces between the tongues of fire, and he moved by an instinct honed through years of confronting this nemesis, of having to assess, in a matter of seconds, the likely and unlikely paths those fiery tongues would take. The two of them finally got to her. They lifted the beams one by one. They pulled her out and carried her to safety outside.

He then hobbled hastily to Snow's restaurant, his anxiety escalating by the minute. The three-storey building housing her restaurant had collapsed. He heard a moan from somewhere inside the rubble. Frantic, he crawled into the wreckage towards the sound, the way he had crawled into the collapsed Hotel New World.

As he got closer to the voice, he could see the legs of a woman. Her foot had been blown off, and her leg was bleeding profusely. He could not see her face. He edged forward a little more, pushing the debris aside carefully till he could see her more clearly. She was delirious. But it was not his wife. It was Komala, his wife's employee.

There was no sign of anyone else. The customers had probably left by the time of the blast. Slowly, he pulled Komala out onto the road. An Indonesian taxi driver was standing nearby. Yang called out to him. '*Abang! Pergi hospital, boleh*? Brother! Go to the hospital, can?'

The man shouted back, '*Boleh!* Can!'

They put Komala into the taxi. As it sped its way to the hospital, he turned back towards the wreckage, panting. His clothes were soaked in perspiration and blood. His mind was soaked in dread. He searched the area furiously, desperately.

There was no sign of her.

He reached into his shirt pocket for his mobile phone; he had to try all means of reaching her, however remote the chances were. But his phone was not in his pocket; it must have fallen out when he was thrown to the ground by the powerful impact of the bomb blast, or when he was crawling in the wreckage trying to reach Komala.

The fire at the Sari Club blazed on. He went back, trying to help the locals and tourists who were attempting to reach the victims. But without fire hoses and fire suits, there was only so much they could do, their efforts thwarted by the flames and the heat. Although they could hear more screams coming from the back of the building, they could not reach them. They could only watch helplessly as those still trapped in the burning building were burned to death.

The police, firefighters and paramedics arrived. They took over the search and rescue operations. Firefighters began putting out the fire.

He searched for her, his heart alternating between racing and stopping as he came across more bodies. More body parts. All around him, there were cries of anguish from those with parts of their bodies blown off, from those with parts of their skin blackened, from those searching for family or friend, from those who found family or friend. Charred. Killed.

He searched, feeling as if he were going mad. What was she wearing? Skirt? Pants? What colour? He could not remember, could not even remember what his wife was wearing. He saw a woman lying face down on the street. He stopped breathing; heaved at her body, turning her over. It was not her. He breathed. He went to another body. Once more he stopped breathing. He looked at the face. He breathed again.

He hobbled again to what was once her restaurant. He stood on the street facing the wreckage, hopeful and despairing all at once. He could not find her. That could mean that she was somewhere else, safe. Or it could mean that some of those body parts on the street were hers.

Dark feathers of thick smoke continued to rise on outstretched wings, carrying with them his silent prayer to the heavens above.

He saw again the colossal yellow tsunami forty-one years ago which had altered their lives, his and hers, forever. He saw again the flames he had fought time and again in the line of duty; the wreckage of the Hotel New World, beneath which he had dug, and after which their paths—his path and hers—had crossed again.

He heard her singing once again in the mango tree when they had first met. He heard her sobbing beneath the cold shower at 5 a.m. that morning.

He felt again the touch of her hand, her lips, her body, soft and warm in its caress, yet bold and unflinching in bearing his brokenness.

Had their lives, everything that they had been through, come to this?

His stomach clenched into a fist—a helpless, cornered fist which, unable to hit out in anger at another, could only punch inward, effecting what pain it could with each strike, till he was brought down on one knee. On the wounded, bleeding knee. Beads of sweat glistened on his forehead. Tears singed his eyes.

With monumental effort, he heaved himself off the ground. He continued searching.

Chapter 49

Through the evening of that fateful day, Snow had hardly had a moment to spare as customers streamed endlessly into the restaurant. She lost track of the time. When she finally managed to sit down with a glass of water in hand, it was already 10.40 p.m.

Then, something strange happened. She heard her mother's voice. *Xue'er*, Ma seemed to be calling her. She sat up; looked around, baffled. Ma was a long way from here, in Bandung. How was it that she was hearing Ma's voice?

Xue'er. There it was again.

She searched in her bag for her mobile phone. It was not there. Where had she left it? She searched the drawer at the payment counter. Not there either. Finally, she found her phone in the kitchen; she had, for some reason, left it in the kitchen on this busy night.

There were two missed calls on her phone. Her mother had tried to reach her at 9.45 p.m. and again at 10 p.m. She had to return her mother's calls. With several customers talking loudly in the restaurant, she stepped out onto Jalan Legian with her phone. The ruckus on the street was, however, equally bad, if not worse, what with the throngs of people there. She walked towards Kuta beach.

It was 11 p.m. by the time she reached Kuta beach, where she made the phone call to Bandung. Her uncle picked up the call. He told her that her mother had already gone to bed. She said she would call again in the morning, and they hung up.

She tarried at the beach, sitting for some minutes, feeling the gusty breath of the ocean. Then, suddenly, the earth shook.

The pockets of people on Kuta beach swivelled around when what sounded like an earthquake rocked the island. The earth tremored for a few seconds. As they stared landward, a huge ball of fire ballooned into the air, coughing out billows of black smoke. A collective gasp emanated from the beach.

Snow stood stunned. For a few moments, those at the beach stood gaping at the spectacle further inland, unsure what to make of it. Then someone exclaimed, 'Was that an explosion?'

She gasped. Yang was supposed to meet her at her restaurant at just about this time. If it was really an explosion, he and Komala would have been in the thick of it.

Her thoughts went wild. She took out her mobile phone, fumbling in her frenzy as she clumsily pressed the numbers. There was a ring, but no answer. She tried again. Still no answer. With her heart beating violently, she ran towards the town.

Her breath caught itself in its own tumultuous haste as she raced back to the restaurant. The annihilation that met her eyes as she approached Jalan Legian was unlike anything she had ever seen before. She stopped running. Her stomach began to churn as she stepped over human hands and fingers, over bodies with no legs, or legs with no bodies. Glass and wood fragments lodged themselves in the soles of her shoes.

She stood, dumbstruck, facing her restaurant. Nothing was left. A horrific blaze had gutted the nearby Sari Club, where locals and tourists were racing against time, flames, and heat to save those trapped inside. She looked around. There was no sign of Komala. And no sign of Yang.

Injured people were lying or sitting on the street amid the mayhem. She searched desperately among them, going from one to another. She made her way down towards the Sari Club. The local firefighters were directing their jets of water at the large inferno, attempting to put out the flames. Policemen were there. Paramedics were attending to the injured victims.

She searched frantically for Yang and Komala along the street. A young girl lay on one side, her body charred, her eyes no longer seeing. Not far from her lay the body of a man, burnt beyond recognition. All around them lay body parts, some blackened, others bloody. The entire place, bustling and alive just minutes ago, now reeked of death and destruction.

A Caucasian man, tall and muscular, sat on the pavement, sobbing. Beside him lay the body of another man, half his head blown off by the explosion. An Indonesian woman was walking the streets, crying, calling out, 'Siti … Siti …' Snow walked up to this woman, reaching out to touch her on the arm. Their eyes met in the common sorrow of a fallen humanity. They held each other for a while, then both women resumed their agonizing search.

She stood there, frozen for a moment, trying to breathe. She felt as if she would retch. How could one make sense of what was happening? Of what had just happened?

She began walking slowly, almost in a daze, her feet trudging along. Tears began to singe her eyes. Those body parts, those charred bodies. That they could be his sent a chill down her spine so unbearable, she wanted to scream.

She looked around her, at the faces of the bleeding men and women sitting on the street, at the bodies of dead men and women lying on the ground.

Then, she saw a figure further down the road. She could not see his face; his back was facing her as he hobbled in the opposite direction, away from her. She ran. She called out to him. He turned around.

They stood facing each other. She was panting, from running as much as from relief. He, too, was breathless, as the person he had desperately been searching for now stood before him.

His jeans were soaked in blood from the deep gash on his leg. His hands were covered in lacerations. His lips were pale from the loss of blood.

As relief softened the tension in his body, his injured leg buckled, and he fell on his knees to the ground.

Chapter 50

She ran forward, knelt facing him, her hands holding onto his arms. His palms were pressed onto the glass fragments on the ground, supporting the weight of his frame even as the glass cut into them.

He looked up at her, her face now close. He could see the wetness in her eyes.

'I was ... so afraid ... afraid you ...' he panted as he struggled to hold on to the energy that was quickly draining away.

'Me too,' she said softly. 'Me too.'

'Where were you? Are you hurt?'

'I'm okay. I was at the beach.'

'Komala's at the hospital. I found her. One foot was blown off. But she's alive.'

'Thank you,' she choked.

Their foreheads touching, she held his hands in hers, so that his weight bore down on her rather than on the glass-strewn ground. He brought one hand up to her cheek, feeling the warmth of her face, relishing the real, living presence of one so beloved, whom he had come so close to losing.

As they knelt there holding each other in a moment of pure thankfulness at being alive, all the years of separation, of heartache and loneliness, of losing faith in themselves and in their love, seemed to sluice out from the depths of their being, unshackling the doubts and hurts and inhibitions which had held them apart for so long.

She gathered herself. 'I have to get you to the clinic. You're losing too much blood.'

She looped his arm around her shoulder, supporting him as he struggled to get up, as they hobbled towards the 24-hour clinic near Kuta beach.

Chaos greeted them at the clinic. The place was overflowing with people injured in the explosion. Many had shrapnel wounds like Yang's; some had small patches of burnt skin hanging loose; others had more serious injuries such as wounds to the head or severe burns on their bodies. They were lying or sitting on the floor, in the corridor, or any place they could fit into.

The clinic was not equipped to handle such a large-scale catastrophe; it did not have sufficient staff, nor medical instruments and supplies. Antiseptic, gauze, bandages, and the like were running out. Overwhelmed medical staff attended to those with more serious injuries first, some of whom had to be sent to the hospital. The locals enlisted the help of more locals to bring these victims to the hospital in their vehicles; those who had ferried victims to the hospital remarked that the hospital was equally overwhelmed.

It was close to 3 a.m. by the time a nurse was able to attend to Yang. The doctor had to remove the glass shards embedded in his wound before stitching it up; twenty stitches in all were required to close the wound.

Dawn was almost breaking by the time they returned to his hotel room. When they had recovered a little, they sat looking out of the window at the vastness of the ocean beyond Kuta Bay. She told him why she had gone to the beach. That she had heard her mother's voice, had seen the missed calls on her phone, had gone out to return her mother's calls. That had saved her.

They tuned in to the news on the radio. People all over the world were beginning to hear of the three bombs that had been detonated in Bali—one by a suicide bomber in Paddy's Bar, the second and most deadly one outside the Sari Club from a van loaded with explosives, and a third, smaller one near the US and the Australian Consulates which caused no injuries. The first bomb had sent people fleeing from Paddy's Bar out onto the street, where the much more lethal second bomb was waiting for them. More than a hundred people had been confirmed dead, with the death toll still rising as people were reported missing and bodies were being identified. Responsibility for the attacks seem to point towards the extremist Jemaah Islamiyah (JI).

As the news gave way to music over the radio, they sat wordlessly, almost in stupor; Snow, shaken, unable to get the images of the carnage out of her head; Yang, silent, hearing over and over again the screams of the people trapped in the Sari Club inferno. He drew his arms around her, and they sat in the company of trauma, of relief, of grief; two souls who thanked the heavens that they were still alive, who shed tears for those no longer alive, and who would live with the ordeal of this night for as long as they would remain alive.

In the morning, Snow gave a call to Bandung, to let her Ma and uncle know that she and Yang were safe. Her uncle picked up the call.

'Hold on, I'll go to Su Mei's room to call her,' he told her.

She sensed in her uncle's voice a tinge of curiosity as to why her Ma was still asleep at this hour when she would normally have been up and about. An unexplained disquiet began gnawing at Snow. The voice of her Ma, which she had heard the night before, and the missed calls her Ma had made to her phone came back to her, swirling about in her mind with a nervous energy.

She waited, holding on to the phone for what seemed like an eternity. Her anxiety grew. Why was her uncle taking so long? Why was Ma taking so long?

Finally, her uncle was back on the line. He was almost breathless, his voice frantic. 'Su Mei won't wake up! I kept knocking. I opened the door. She was lying on her bed. She looked so calm, so peaceful, like she was sleeping. I kept on calling her name. Then I touched her hand,' he paused, as if almost unable to believe what had just happened, what he was about to say. 'Her hand was cold.'

Snow slumped onto the sofa beside the telephone. The phone receiver fell from her hand, dangling and swinging by its cord from the small side table. Yang picked it up. He held her as her body went limp.

How could it be? Ma was not ill, did not have any known sickness other than the common flu. How could she have gone so suddenly? Why had she heard Ma's voice at the restaurant; why had she felt Ma's presence, sensed a vague unease that was, at the same time, comforting?

In the numbness of her hazy consciousness, she heard Yang speak into the phone; 'Yes, yes, call a doctor quickly,' he said; the phone being put down, being picked up again. 'Hello, I need two urgent tickets to Bandung please,' and the phone was put down again; a warm touch on her cold hands—why was she feeling so cold?—and a voice, his voice, so distant she could not make out what he was saying, sounding all gibberish; now a shrill sound, a ringing, like a punctuated alarm buzzing away; Yang lifting the phone, 'Hello, uncle, yes we'll be there this afternoon, how about the doctor? On the way? Okay, let us know.'

Now Yang was sitting beside her—for what was there to say to her?—and there was just the sound of the TV, of a woman talking and images of a bomb-devastated Kuta on the screen; faces of people crying in anguish; the woman speaking of hundreds being killed and injured in a chilling act of violence, of injured people who were being flown to Australia or Singapore where they could hopefully be saved; more images of bloodied people with no hands or legs; some important person—a president or prime minister of some country—appearing on the screen with a solemn face and firm voice, so firm it bruised the aching heart, uttering words of condemnation, no, of condolences, looking straight out at her, his gaze unflinching as he said, the world stands in solidarity with you, we are sorry for your loss, we feel for your loss.

And then the damn alarm went off again; those cold, mechanical buzzes whose purpose was to tell you your time was up; time's up my dear; but perhaps the ringing, if it persevered, might be a saviour yet, calling Ma out of slumber; wake up, please wake up; and Yang was shutting it up all too soon, his voice going, 'Hello uncle, the doctor came? What did he say?'

She felt his hands gently holding her shoulders, saw him looking into her face, heard his voice uttering tender words.

'The doctor has confirmed,' he said, 'Ma has passed away; she died peacefully in her sleep last night.'

She felt herself shaking in his grip, and a small, sad voice muttered, *she came, to save me. To say goodbye.*

Chapter 51

Bandung, a week later

Yang and Snow sat in the garden of her family home along Jalan Sumber Mulya, where Ma used to spend her days. In a few hours, they would be boarding a flight headed back to Singapore. They were going home.

The early morning sunlight danced in the droplets of water left on the leaves by the rain that had showered on them during the night. The light scent of ripened mangoes hanging from the mango tree rode on the heavier smell of the soil enfolding them in the garden.

Her Ma had sat here for a long time on that last night, her uncle had said. On that night of the Bali bombing. The night her Ma had saved her.

She began to cry. He reached over, held her hand.

As they sat there, a rainbow appeared, as if bridging the end of the earth with the beginning of the sky. From the sunlight gliding through the droplets of rain, the glorious smile of nature reached out from the earth into the wind and the clouds above, gifting them with a moment of unspeakable beauty. The world wore a fleeting happiness in the space between the sun and the rain, the earth and the sky. In the manner of all things in between, one could not grasp it, could not keep it. The only way we could hold on to it was in that other in-between space we call our hearts.

She turned to him, smiling through her tears.

Her hand rested in his, near the wound on his leg just above his knee. She gazed at the long cut on his skin, now sewn together by the many threads. She looked at the scar on his neck from the burns he sustained in the line of duty. She gazed into the scars of her own heart and, from there, into his.

The fresh wound on his leg was healing, but the scar would remain with him, on him—a mark of what he had been through, of who he was, and what defined his life. An inscription of the past on the present. Of the present on the future.

Perhaps, a scar was simply a statement of imperfection in our very imperfect world. A visible statement stamped onto our bodies, or an invisible one burned into our hearts.

Their scars would never go away, but her mother had made peace with her scars. It could have taken a year, or maybe ten years. Twenty perhaps. Or a lifetime.

And as she sat with him beneath the rainbow, she saw her mother once again, bearing her imperfections on her face, smiling at them.

***** End *****

Author's Note

Indonesia's worst terror attack in its history took place in Kuta, Bali, on 12 October 2002. The final death toll stood at 202 people; hundreds more were injured. Among those killed were people of over twenty nationalities, mostly foreigners, but also including many locals. As investigations into the massacre began, many of the injured victims were flown to Australia or to regional countries like Singapore for medical treatment. Many suffered severe burns, requiring months of hospital treatment, painful surgeries, and skin grafts, as well as years of rehabilitation. Some survived. Others succumbed to their injuries. Those who survived with serious injuries would never fully recover, having to live their lives without a limb or with burn scars on their bodies. Hundreds more would have to live with the sudden loss of a loved one.

The Bukit Ho Swee fire, which occurred on 25 May 1961, was the worst fire in Singapore's history since World War II. It razed a 100-acre area (0.4 sq km) consisting of a school, shops, factories, and wooden and attap houses, claiming four lives, injuring about 50, and rendering some 15,000 kampong dwellers homeless. The cause of the fire remains unknown. The fire was a pivotal moment in the development of modern Singapore with its public housing program.

Acknowledgments

My appreciation to Nora Nazerene Abu Bakar, Ishani Bhattacharya, and the team at Penguin Random House Southeast Asia, for bringing books from this region to the world.

To the victims, and their families, of the Bali bombing, the Hotel New World collapse, and the Bukit Ho Swee fire—this book is written in honour of you.

To the firefighters and disaster relief personnel all around the world, who risk life and limb to save others—thank you.

To burn victims and their families, whose painful and difficult recovery is often unseen and not well understood—I hope this book tells you how brave you are.

Thank you to my mum and my sister for your love, and to Hazel, Meira, Tara, and all my friends who have believed in me.

My love to my husband and children. Thank you for your unconditional love.

Glossary

Abang	*Brother* in Malay
Ah-Yee	*Aunty* in Chinese
Alamak	A Malay exclamation of surprise or dismay
Bapak	*Father* in Malay
Boleh	*Can* in Malay
Chantek	*Beautiful* in Malay
Char Kway Teow	Flat rice noodles fried with black sauce
Cheh	An exclamation of exasperation or disdain
Chio	Pretty
Dai Kah Jie	*Eldest sister* in Cantonese

Dai kor	*Older brother* in Cantonese
Dimana	*Where* in Malay
HDB	Housing and Development Board
Ibu	*Mother* in Malay
Ji Lang	A person who herds chickens in Chinese
Kay-poh	Slang for being nosy
Lelong	*Sale* in Malay
Long kor	*Big brother Dragon* in Chinese
Longkang	A small drain
Luwak	Small civet native to Bali and other parts of Asia
Mari	*Come* in Malay
Makan	*Eat* in Malay
Martabak Manis	A sweet pancake popular in Indonesia
Nasi Padang	Rice with various dishes
Nenek	*Grandmother* in Malay
Ni Hao	*Hope you're well* in Chinese
Niu Lang	*Cowherd* in Chinese

San fu	*Hard life* in Cantonese
Sayang	A Malay word of endearment and love
Tow Kay	*Boss* in Hokkien
Yee Kah Jie	*Second sister* in Cantonese